New to the Game

Lock Down Publications and Ca$h
Presents
New to the Game
A Novel by *Malik D. Rice*

Lock Down Publications
P.O. Box 870494
Mesquite, Tx 75187

Copyright 2020 by Malik D. Rice
New to the Game

First Edition March 2020
Printed in the United States of America

This is a work of fiction. Names, characters, places, and incidents either are products of the author's imagination or are used fictitiously. Any similarity to actual events or locales or persons, living or dead, is entirely coincidental.

Lock Down Publications
Like our page on Facebook: Lock Down Publications @
www.facebook.com/lockdownpublications.ldp
Cover design and layout by: **Dynasty Cover Me**
Book interior design by: **Shawn Walker**
Edited by: **Sunny Giovani**

Stay Connected with Us!

Text **LOCKDOWN** to 22828 to stay up-to-date with new releases, sneak peaks, contests and more…

Thank you!

Submission Guideline.

Submit the first three chapters of your completed manuscript to ldpsubmissions@gmail.com, subject line: Your book's title. The manuscript must be in a .doc file and sent as an attachment. Document should be in Times New Roman, double spaced and in size 12 font. Also, provide your synopsis and full contact information. If sending multiple submissions, they must each be in a separate email.

Have a story but no way to send it electronically? You can still submit to LDP/Ca$h Presents. Send in the first three chapters, written or typed, of your completed manuscript to:

LDP: Submissions Dept
P.O. Box 870494
Mesquite, Tx 75187

DO NOT send original manuscript. Must be a duplicate.

Provide your synopsis and a cover letter containing your full contact information.

Thanks for considering LDP and Ca$h Presents.

Malik D. Rice

CHAPTER 1
~Rampage~

"You don't feel it yet?"

"Feel what?"

"The soul slipping out of your body."

I looked over at Kapo with slanted eyes and a straight face. He was a big homie in the hood, and I was grateful that he cared enough to take me up under his wing and all, but he was killing me with all the philosophical shit. He had to get deep on every subject, we could never just have a regular conversation. But then again, we weren't regular niggas.

"No, nigga. The only thing I feel comin' out my body is heat. You got a nigga takin' a stroll through the park in the middle of December. My dick in my stomach right now."

"For a coldblooded youngin like yourself, it shouldn't be a problem."

I shook my head at his bad attempt at a joke. "Did you actually want somethin' when you called me out here? Or did you just feel like hearing yourself preach?"

"I'm actually wondering why I even bother wasting my time with yo lil' sarcastic ass, but I called you out here for a reason. I got a job for you."

"Now you talkin' my lingo." I stated while rubbing my hands together in prayer-position. Kapo was a kingpin, so if he had a job for me it was worth it.

Kapo took a seat on a bench, but I remained standing. It was too cold for all that shit. "One of my spots got hit about a month ago, but I'm just now finding out who was behind it."

"Who?"

"JD and his daddy. I'm guessing he done let his pops get in his head and trick him into committing suicide."

"Damnnnn, JD." JD was a mid-level dealer in Kapo's camp, and the father to one of my favorite cousin's child, that he took care of. I would hate to see something happen to him, but if he really did what Kapo said, his ass was grass. "You sure?"

Kapo nodded his head. "Positive. Your cousin fucked around and told her aunt about JD coming home one night with a lot of money and drugs. More money than she ever saw him with. But she didn't know that her aunt had her on speakerphone, or that her aunt's best friend was with her, which is my right-hand-man's side hoe."

"Damn, shawty, so what you want me to do? Whack the nigga?"

"Not immediately. Snatch him up, tie him up, and beat the truth out of him. I want to know *everybody* involved. Then kill him, and everybody that had something to do with it. I'm trying to make an example out of this situation."

"What's the ticket?"

He stood up and knotted his brow thinking on a good number. "I'll give you ten a pop."

"His ass is grass for ten thousand dollars, and I hope it was seven niggas with 'em. I'll handle this shit personally."

The next thing I knew, I felt his hand slapping me on the back of the head.

"You don't listen to shit that come out of my mouth, do you? You a Don now. Not only are you labeled untouched, you're labeled non-active. Meaning you are not to get your hands dirty. That's what you got Mafiosos and Mobsters for. You got to start moving like a boss; you not a shooter no more, Rampage."

"I got you, big bro. I'll get it done."

Thirty minutes later, I was pulling up to McNair High School on Bouldercrest Road to pick up both of my sisters. Usually I would have somebody to pick them up every day from school in one of my Escalades, but I promised to pick them up personally every Friday. I tried my best to keep my promises to family.

They tried to make me promise not to pull up with the four shooters that were following me in another Escalade, but that was my kill team and I wasn't going anywhere in public without them. I had a $50,000 bounty on my head from that OG I whacked on the westside, and I wasn't taking any chances.

I saw them come out of the main building together like I told them. My right-hand-man, Toe-Tag, hopped out of the driver's seat, walked around the truck and waited for them. When they got to the truck, he greeted them and opened the door for them so they could get in the back with me.

"Heyyyy, brotherrrr!" Kamya sang after getting in the car. She was my older sister and loved me to death; she loved everybody. She was one of the sweetest people on earth, but she wasn't the brightest star in the sky. I always joked, saying her daddy was a preacher or some shit.

"Wassup, baby girl? How was yo' day?"

"It was good." She answered cheerfully.

My younger sister, Babie, rolled her eyes. "That girl lyin' like hell. She came to me cryin' today because a girl had called her slow in the hallway."

"Why the fuck y'all ain't jump that hoe? Where she at? Stop the car, Toe-Tag!" Everybody knew how I was about my family, especially my sisters. I would slap an old lady for disrespecting one of them.

Kamya got frightened and her pretty hazel eyes got big. She wrapped both arms round me and held me as tight as she could. "Noooo, Ray! Just leave it alone. She was just playing."

"That's why we ain't jump the bitch. She always trying to save somebody." Barbie chimed in with her little arms crossed. She was a cute baby doll on the outside, but on the inside, she shared the same demons as me. We had the same father.

"Who is it, Babie?"

She turned around in her seat and looked back at me sideways. "Nigga, you don't think I would've been suspended already if she would've pointed the hoe out?"

"Yeah, you got a point." I looked down at Kamya. "You need to stop lettin' folks hurt yo' feelings, girl. You know me and Babie don't play 'bout you."

She let me go and sat up right in her seat. "I know, and I love y'all so much... Just don't want y'all to get in trouble because of me."

People started bumping their horn's behind us. We were holding up traffic. "What you want me to do, bro?" Toe-Tag asked me.

"Let's ride. We got to drop them off; got a busy night ahead of us."

***

Lisa was a twenty-three-year-old stripper that was all about her business. She was a light-bright amazon with a coke bottle figure, and a cool personality to go with it. JD lucked-up when he won her heart, and he lucked-up when Kapo decided to stamp him, but his luck had just run out.

I watched as Lisa came out of the nail salon on Candler Road, and I watched as Toe-Tag approached her and escorted her over to the truck. "Cuzzo, wassam?" I greeted as she climbed in.

"Boy, you done got a few stripes and went Hollywood."

"The Don wanna see you."

"Boy, stop! You still my lil' cute ass cousin. Wassup tho'?"

I looked down at my new Rolex. "I'm up, fuck you mean?"

"Yeah, yeah. I seen you doin' good, baby. I'm proud of you."

"I 'preciate that, cuzzo. Look though, I ain't got too much time to spare. I'm just trynna see if you know where yo' baby daddy at. Niggas in y'all apartments said they ain't seen him around lately."

"Him and his daddy went to Miami to visit some extended family out there, or something. Why? Wassup? What he do?"

I nodded my head casually. She just told me everything I needed to know. "He ain't do shit. Kapo just gave that nigga some stripes and wanted me to tell him."

Her eyes lit up. "JD a made man now?"

"Hell nah. He got bumped up to Mafioso-two though. Don't tell him. Wait 'til he get back so it can be a surprise."

"Okay." She started gathering her shopping bags so she could leave.

"Here. Buy you and Lil' Mamma somethin' nice." I handed her $500 before she got out.

"Okay, I will. Love you, Ray."

"Love you too, baby girl."

Four hours later, I woke up to gunshots in my neighborhood. Eagle Run Apartments was a violent place, and I was used to the gunshots, but it was the devastating female screech that came soon after that I wasn't used to. I was one-hundred-forty-four percent sure that everybody in the hood heard her.

At first, I rolled over thinking if AK needed me to handle some business, he'll send for me. It wasn't that late, it was only ten o'clock, but the Lean I was sipping earlier had me out of it. Then I popped up with my eyes wide open and remembered something. AK wouldn't be sending for me because I took his spot. He wasn't responsible for what happened in the hood anymore, I was.

I got up and got dressed as fast as I could. By the time I was out of my spot and down the stairs, my kill team was just walking up to my building. "What the fuck just happened?" I asked Black as he approached.

"Maniac caught Tammy's freaky ass givin' one of them Duct Tape niggas some head in his car and snapped. He snatched his strap out his pocket and blessed both of 'em."

"Damn, shawty!" Not only was this a nightmare, it was a nightmare that happened on my turf, so it was my problem because Maniac was in my camp.

Maniac was twenty-four, the second oldest person in my camp. Most of the older niggas in the hood left, complaining about how the young niggas were making it too hot, and Maniac was a big portion of that temperature. He put you in the mind of the actor Idris Elba by the looks, and O-Dogg from *Menace 2 Society* by the personality. He was one helluva nigga, and this nigga Vonte thought it was a good idea to make me responsible for him and all the rest of the maniacs in my camp. Most of 'em older than me.

"Popped they ass right in from of Ms. May spot. You know how much she love her granddaughter." Black's little brother, G-Baby, chimed in. He was a loyal nigga if he fucked with you, so I kept him around for obvious reason.

We heard sirens approaching from a distance and stepped back into the breezeway. "I'm surprised that old lady screamed like that without giving herself a heart-attack. Where Toe-Tag and Monster at?"

Everybody shrugged.

CHAPTER 2
~ Toe-Tag ~

Vonte did the right thing when he made my nigga Rampage a made man. Me and Rampage been niggas since we were sucking on our mothers' titties, so if he was in position, I was in position. AK was power-struck and always put bullshit in the game, so that's what he got out of it. It's funny because one day me and Rampage was talking about how we'll never be on bullshit like him if we ever made it to that level, but it was really wishful thinking. We never thought that one of us would actually take his spot.

When Rampage got in position, he bumped me up to Mafioso-four right up under him and told me that he gone need my help running the camp. Not even two months ago, I was just dreaming about a world where I could support my son and my family. Now I sat in the driver's seat of my new black-on-black 2014 Hellcat Dodge Charger with purple interior. I had $8,000 in 20's on my lap, and a Dope Boy Rolex on my wrist. I always wondered how I'd feel once I made it this far, but now that I was here, I couldn't explain the feeling. I didn't know how to feel.

Monster exhaled a thick cloud of weed smoke in the passenger's seat next to me. Then passed the blunt to me. "These niggas need to tighten up. Ain't no way you gone pull up in Eagle Run in no Hellcat without niggas bein' all over that muthafucka." He was my big brother from another mother. One of the most ruthless niggas on the east side.

We were in an apartment complex right off of Wesley Chapel Road. A nigga named Strong ran a crew of niggas that went by the name of Flight Crew. They were building a little name for themselves throughout the city, but they were known for trapping. They were money-makers, not gangsters. That's why we were here.

"You damn right too. These niggas ain't got no security system what-so-ever. Look at 'em. They think this shit a game." A group of block-boys stood on the side of a building serving clientele and joking around. They were in their own little world.

Monster shook his head. "I see."

"Come on." I stuffed my money into my sweatpants, grabbed my mini AK-74, and got out the car.

It was five niggas on the block. Nobody noticed us approaching until we walked into the light of the streetlamp above. "Oh shit!" Two of them took off running behind the building, and the other three froze up like Subzero. I couldn't blame them though. I was 6-feet, and Monster was 6'5". Both of us were stocky niggas dressed in all black, not-to-mention the cannons we had aimed at them.

"Put y'all backs on the wall and spread yo' legs as far as they can go!" I commanded sharply as we closed in on them.

They followed directions with their hands to the sky, even though nobody told them to do that part. Monster chuckled just loud enough for me to hear and I didn't have to guess what he found so funny because I already knew. The niggas looked so scared that they probably would've sucked each other's dicks if we told them to. I could easily tell that all of them were older than me, just like I could tell they weren't about the gunplay.

Monster walked up to the one in the middle and snatched his chain with their logo on it. I aimed the red beam from my gun at his left eyeball. "You must be the nigga in charge right now."

He nodded.

Monster started emptying his pockets.

"You know why we here?"

He nodded. "To rob us."

Monster kicked him in the dick, sending him to the ground howling in pain.

"Wrong answer." I aimed the beam at the fat man to the right. "How 'bout you, Fluffy? You know why we here?"

I could see him breathing through his mouth. It was cold outside, but I doubt that's why he was shaking. He looked down at his partner, over at Monster, then straight at me. He shook his head making his fat cheeks jiggle. "I don't know."

Monster looked at me, and I shrugged my shoulders. He kneed Fluffy in the nuts. Fluffy went down.

I pointed the gun at the last one standing— a short stocky man— and his eyes got bigger than they already were, but he didn't have to worry. He was the lucky one. "Tell Strong he got a message from Dilluminati." Monster put a brand new Trac Phone in his pocket, that we'd just bought and activated. "Give him that phone and tell him we'll be in touch."

I stopped at the four-way on Flat Shoals Road to get some gas at the Citgo. Monster was pumping gas when I finally checked my phone and saw all the missed calls from Rampage. I called him back, and he told me about everything that happened since I been gone. I told him I was around the corner on my way back, then hung up. It's crazy how so much shit could happen in just a few hours.

As soon as I bent down to pick up my lighter off the floor, gunshots rang out and my window shattered. Somebody was trying to take our heads off. I crawled across the seat, opened the passenger's door, and dived out the other side. Monster was squatted with his hand over the trunk, shooting back with his Glock 27 already.

People were running and screaming. I came up with my Draco over the hood of the car trying my best not to hit nobody with a stray bullet. I had tunnel vision on the white Honda. After a few rounds from me and Monster, they swerved out of the parking lot recklessly. We got back in my car and attempted to chase them down, ready to make them suffer for trying us, but they made a right into an apartment complex we called The Hamp, right down the street from the gas station.

"How you know it was them Duct Tape niggas?" Rampage asked me.

Everybody was piled up in Rampage's new apartment. We had a situation on our hands and had to figure out what we were going to do. "Because we got mob-ties wit' PDE and Slaughter Gang, so it got to be them. You know The Hamp they second home anyway."

Rampage let out an aggravated sigh. That Don shit was putting age on my young nigga already. I knew him better than anybody other than his sisters. I knew he was stressing. Big Bag was the Godfather over Duct Tape, and the nigga that Maniac whacked was his son's right-hand-man. "The first nigga to bring Maniac to me get $2,500. Let me chop it up wit' my kill team real quick." Rampage announced, and niggas immediately began clearing the spot out. He was young, but his word was law.

When shit cleared out only me, Monster, Black, Quay, and G-Baby remained. The only nigga missing from the picture was Maniac's crazy ass.

"Wassup, bruh? What you thinkin' 'bout?" I asked.

Rampage ran a hand down his face and slumped even more on the couch. "I'm thinkin' about giving AK his muthafuckin' spot back, that's what I'm thinkin'. I ain't never been this stressed out in my life. It's too much that come wit' this shit."

"I better not neva hear you say no shit like that out yo' mouth again, shawty. You ain't in this shit alone. You got us behind you, we gone get through this shit together."

"I got two options right now. Strike back and start another war, or whack Maniac to make them feel better and avoid a war. I ain't wit' either one." The apartment was quiet for a long while. Everybody was trying to come up with a third option.

Monster breathed a heavily while scratching his bushy beard. "I ain't gone lie, whackin' Maniac is out the question. He done did too much for the hood. That's our brother. We ain't 'bout to whack him 'cause he whacked some other nigga, that's crazy. Fuck them folks."

We all nodded in understanding. Monster's word held a lot of weight. He was twenty-six, the oldest nigga in the camp. And he was making a lot of sense.

I picked my Draco up off the coffee table and stood up from the couch. "Let's crank this shit up then!" It wasn't no need in wasting time.

"Sit yo' ass down, Tee. We still got a procedure we got to follow; we can't just crank no war up like that." Said Rampage.

I glared down at him. "Them niggas just tried to take me and Monster's head off at a muthafuckin' gas station, shawty! Fuck all that."

"And Maniac did the same to theirs first, but the only difference is he ain't miss."

I sat back down with the Draco in my lap. He was making sense, but I was still hot about the situation. "What's the plan then?"

"First, we got to find Maniac and make sure he don't whack nobody else. Then I'ma set a meeting wit' Big Bag's son. What's that nigga name again?" He asked with a crumbled face, rambling through his memory.

"Laroe." Quay answered quickly. "You know he used to fuck wit' one of my big sisters."

Rampage looked at Quay with interest. "Can she still get in touch wit' him?"

"Yeah, she should. She still fuck with his big sister. The one that was in Trouble's video."

"Aight. Tell her to tell him that Don Rampage need to sit down wit' him."

Quay whipped his phone out and went to texting his sister.

"Aye, Tee."

I looked up at him. I probably looked madder than I actually was, but he wasn't going for it.

"Go home to yo' baby mamma. She been blowin' my phone up, cussin' me out talkin' about I'm the reason you ain't been home in three days."

I shook my head. "She might not see me for another three days, it's too much goin' on right now. We got too much to do, bruh."

"We know you loyal and love the family. You been putting in overtime, lil' bruh, go home to yo' family. You ain't gone miss shit. If we need you, we gone come get you." Monster said while looking at me how my big brother used to before he went to prison. He made him a promise that he'd look after me, and he'd been doing just that ever since.

Once again, I couldn't even argue. I have been going hard in these streets, and I did miss my family. I just got so caught up trying to get shit right so I could boss up and take some time off to spend with them, but of course they didn't see things that way.

***

Twenty minutes later, I was sitting in the living room of my apartment with my son in my lap, looking up at my mother and my baby mother, who both stood over me with hands on their hips. They were tag-teaming a nigga. My mother was tripping about money for this and that, and Shanay was tripping about my time.

I sat Lil' Tee next to me, took the bankroll out of my pocket, and gave my mother $400 out of it. "Watch Lil' Tee for me real quick. I got to talk to Shanay in the room real quick."

She put the money in her bra. "That was for bills. I need my hair and nails done."

"Goddamn, man. You'll squeeze a leprechaun out a pot of

gold." I gave her $140 more and hurried up to the room before she got me out my whole damn bankroll.

We almost made it to the room when my little sister, Terri, walked out the room she shared with my mother. "Hey, Tee!" She ran up to me and gave me a hug.

"Wassup, lil' girl? You missed yo' brother?"

She nodded her head. "Yuppp... Can I get some money?"

"Just like yo' goddamn mamma." I gave her $80. "Get out my way."

"I love you too, big head!" She shouted but I closed the door in her face.

Once we were in our room, I sat on the bed, but Shanay just stood there with a hand back on her hip, peering down at me. "What?"

"You must done found you another bitch out there, or something? Before, I couldn't get you off my bra strap, now I got to do the most for yo' attention. Like what the fuck, Tee? I ain't like yo' mamma, I don't care about the money. I need a baby daddy that's gone spend time with me and his child. I really don't care about no other bitch; I just need you to—"

I tuned her ass out and started scanning her body. She wasn't the prettiest bitch around, but she had dimples and sexy lips. What she lacked in the face department her body made up for it. She didn't have a big, stupid booty, but she did have a loose apple booty with cuffs on the bottom. Her c-cups were perfect in my eyes, and her smooth chocolate skin made everything better. You couldn't find a stretch mark on her body. You'd never know that she just had a baby last year. She had on black spandex pants with a white tank-top, and no bra. I started undressing her with my eyes and my dick started rocking up. As soon as I got on full brick, I reached inside my pants and whipped out my yellow sausage.

"Boy, what the fuck?"

I started shaking it back and forth. "This all you want anyway. Come get it."

At first, she stood there hesitantly like she didn't want this shit, then she started taking baby steps toward me. By the time I pulled the hoodie over my head, she was on her knees. If I didn't know nothing else in this life, I knew my dick was her kryptonite.

She grabbed it and started shaking it herself. "I should cut it off, then yo' ass won't have power over me no more." She joked seriously.

"You should swallow it."

She stuck her tongue out and flicked it across the head a few times. If I let her take control of the situation, we'll be going at it forever. She was gone be gentle and slow. I was tired and didn't have time to be wrestling with this girl all night. I wanted to spend time with my son too, so I took control. She was about to get hit with the round-house-special.

About five years ago, Monster taught me and Rampage about the round-house-special and warned us not to use it on a girl unless we wanted her to be in our lives forever. I used it on Shanay's black ass, and she ain't been right ever since.

I stopped her, made her stand up, and take her clothes off while I got rid of the rest of mine. I told her to get back on her knees, and I stood to my feet.

"Oh, shit. Here we go." She whined with her back against the bed, facing me. I knew her juices were flowing, she loved this shit with a passion.

"Shut up." I spat aggressively, grabbed a handful of her weave with one hand, and forced my dick into her mouth with the other.

She grabbed the back of my right thigh with her left hand and played in her pussy with her right one while I fucked her face. She was a woman in public, but behind closed doors, she was my little porn star.

"Daddy missed this throat." She knew how to take dick in every hole on her body. Somehow, she fought her gag reflexes and took as much of my thick 9-inches down her throat as she could.

I sped my strokes up as she looked up at me with tears in her eyes. I felt the sperm dropping from my lower stomach, through my pole, to my tip. I thought about pulling it out so I wouldn't nut so fast, but she'd be insecure about her head-game, so I pinched her nostrils together, forced my dick down as far as it would go, and literally sprayed four days' worth of cum down her throat.

She found a way to swallow it with my dick in her throat. I kept my grip on her nose, making her hold her breath even longer. Then she started flicking her clit with lightning speed, and rolling her eyes in the back of her head "Hmmph. Ummmmm!" She moaned as she made herself cum.

I snatched out of her mouth and let go of her nose at the same time. She took deep breaths as the tears ran down her face. I grabbed the bottom off her face, leaned in and tongue kissed her roughly. Then I looked at her dead in the eyes, drew mucus down from my nose with a nasty sound, and spit it in her mouth. The first ten times, she spit it out and cursed me out, now she just swallowed it like everything else I put in her mouth.

"Come on." I picked her little ass up and dropped her on the bed.

She knew the routine. She got on her elbows and knees with a mean arch in her back making that little pussy of hers stick out. "What you gone do now, bae?" She looked back at me with fire in her eyes, ready for me to put it out.

I got on my knees and went in face-first. Her pussy was still a mess, so I cleaned it up for her, licking her like a lion does their cub. I guess we were making too much noise because my mother turned the stereo on, playing the radio. It never failed. She did that right on time because when I stuck my tongue in her asshole and started rotating it with three fingers in and out of her pussy, she went bananas.

"Uhhhhh! Fuck! Daddy, you so damnnn nasty!"

I kept that up until she came again, then gave her what she was waiting for. I wrapped the sheet around her neck and tied a knot in the back. I wrapped it around my hand tightly and rammed myself inside of her. She was learning how to take my dick better, but I would always be too much for her. My stroke game was superb.

I popped my thumb in her ass and yanked back on the leash so it could choke her harder as I began pumping harder. "You missed this dick? This what you want?"

"Yessss, nigga! Yes! This my dick!" She growled savagely while throwing that ass back at me. I loved when she fucked a nigga back.

I pulled out her pussy and stuck it in her ass. She tried to run, but I wasn't going for it. I stroked her long and strong, and about two minutes later, I was cumming home. "Damnnnn, shawty!" I let go in her ass and collapsed on the bed lazily.

When she caught her breath, she climbed on top of me. "What you doin'? Nigga, you ain't 'bout to tap-out on me. You gone finish what you started. I looked up at her with the sheet still tied around her neck and laughed.

Her face crumbled. "What's so funny?" She asked while massaging my dick, trying to get it back hard.

"I done turned yo' ass out, shawty. You got that look in yo' eyes like you 'bout to rape a nigga."

She shrugged her shoulders. "You done raped me plenty of times."

"You hell." I grabbed her ass cheeks and lifted her up onto my wood.

We fucked like animals for the rest of the night. I didn't get to spend time with Lil' Tee until the next morning after I fed Shanay her breakfast dick.

Malik D. Rice

CHAPTER 3
~ Jasmine ~

I was in the bed laying down trying to go to sleep. I had school in the morning, and I wasn't trying to be late. The principal told me if I kept coming late he was going to suspend me, and I wasn't trying to hear my mother's mouth. She liked to preach, and I wasn't trying to hear it. The pastor did enough of that on Sunday at church.

As soon as I felt myself drifting off, my phone started ringing. I didn't plan on answering it but I still wanted to know who was calling me so late so I could curse they asses out tomorrow, so I picked the phone up and looked at the screen. It was Rampage. I was surprised to see his name on my call list. We used to be close as hell, but I haven't heard from him since my best friend Adalis got killed. After that, I didn't talk to him, but I kept up with him through all the shit I was hearing about him in the streets.

I answered the phone. He told me to get dressed and meet him outside. He was parked down the street from my house. You would never know I was just on my way to sleep by the way I popped up and found something to wear. I couldn't go out there looking any type of way.

About twenty minutes later, after checking to see if my mother was sleep and creeping down the stairs, I had finally made it out the house. I saw two Escalades across the street, three houses down, and knew that was him. A big ass light skinned nigga with a thick beard opened the back door to the first truck as I walked up. I thanked him as I climbed in. He just nodded his head, closed the door behind me, and got back in the driver's seat.

"Took you long enough. You must took a shower or somethin'?" He asked after taking his Ray Ban's off and looking at me with those sexy eyes of his.

"I had to get dressed and sneak out the house. You know how

my mamma is. You stop talking to me for damn-near two months, now you pop-up in front of my house at two o'lock in the morning out of nowhere. What's up with that?"

He shook his head with a sad look in his eyes. "Ever since Adalis got killed, shit ain't been the same for me. I done been through so much shit it ain't even funny."

"I know. I been hearing a lot about you, plus I been keeping up with yo' Twitter and IG. What's up tho'? Why you wait until now to call me, Ray? What's going' on? You okay?"

He shook his head.

"What's wrong?" I asked in my baby voice with a hand now on his knee. Everybody knew Rampage, but I knew Raylo Brown. He only showed a few people his other side, and fortunately for me, I was one of them. Just like him and Adalis, we had a special bond.

"I live by myself now. You know I can't cook, so I been spendin' way too much on fast food, and I just bought a pit bull puppy that I don't like leavin' at the house. Plus, I don't like sleepin' by myself."

I snatched my hand back and looked at him blankly. "What you saying?"

"Read between the lines, stupid ass lil' girl. I need you to move in wit' me. My sisters ain't trying to leave they mamma, so I'm all alone."

He caught me off guard. I wasn't expecting this at all. Like, was he serious? He wasn't the type to play too many games, so I knew he wasn't, but it still felt unreal. "I mean, you know I wanna move in with you, nigga, but I can't. I got school, and plus my mamma ain't gone go for that shit. You know that."

"You grown, fuck school. And I'll handle yo' mamma." He retorted matter-of-factly.

"Just because you sixteen going on thirty don't mean everybody else is. I'm sixteen going on nineteen at the most. I ain't gone be able to keep up with yo' lifestyle. Plus, I don't want to end up like Adalis." I said that last sentence with a heavy heart.

Me, Adalis and Rampage all grew up together. Rampage and Adalis had always been lovers. Me and Adalis had always been best friends. Me and Rampage had always been fake siblings, but that's just how we played it in public. Behind doors we'd been lovers ever since the seventh grade. Ever since then, he'd been the love of both of our lives.

He reached in the ashtray, grabbed a half-smoked blunt, and set fire to it. We sat in silence for a few uncomfortable minutes, both of us running through our thoughts. "Guess what?" He finally said. I looked up at him. He exhaled a healthy cloud of smoke and passed me the blunt. "It took me a while, but I was layin' down high as fuck one night and finally figured it out."

"Spit—" I started choking on the smoke from the strong weed. "It out nigga!"

"God took Adalis away from me because she was too good for me, but you? He gone let me have you 'cause, like me, you ain't shit. We perfect for each other."

I was so surprised he just said that out his mouth, but it was crazy because it made perfect sense to me too. Shit, I felt the exact same way. Adalis ain't been nothing but good to me, the best friend you could ever ask for, and I repaid her by fucking her nigga. I didn't deserve her either. Ray was right, I ain't shit. "I can't even argue with that."

He tried to pass me the blunt back, but I declined. I didn't want to get stuck to where I couldn't function.

"I know you can't because you know I'm right. So, what you gone do? Go in there and pack yo' shit, write yo' mamma a note telling her you gone be alright, and come to Dinero World wit' daddy?"

I don't know if it was the weed, the fat dick in his pants, the money and clout that I knew would come with being by his side, or the little white-gold diamond DG chain he just pulled out his jacket pocket, but I snatched the chain out of his hand, put it on, and did exactly as he instructed. I didn't know exactly what to expect of my future now, but I did know one thing for certain. My life would *never* be average again.

***

The sky was pitch black with bright stars floating perfectly in their perfect spots. I laid on my stomach looking out at the busy ocean water. Even though I couldn't see past the shore, I heard the water shifting and crashing into itself. I wasn't laying on a towel, so I enjoyed the feeling of the grainy sand on my body.

At first, I thought I heard somebody crying in the distance, but it was faint. The wind was blowing, and the water was moving, so I couldn't really be sure. The sound went away, and I went back to my thoughts of a perfect future with Raylo. A few minutes later, I heard the same crying voice, but this time it was closer, and I actually saw somebody sitting by the water with their back to me.

I got up and walked toward the person. It sounded like a female or a child's voice, but I couldn't be sure because they sat balled up with some kind of white robe on.

"You okay?" I asked as I closed in on them so I wouldn't scare them, but they just kept on crying. I walked up to them and grabbed their shoulder. They turned around with lightning speed. By the time they were facing me they were somehow on their feet right in my face, but I couldn't see them because the hood covered too much of their face. Something told me to take the hood off, so I reached my hand out and slowly removed the hood. "What the fuck?" I jumped back a step with wide eyes and no breath in my lungs. "Adalis... Is that really you?" I asked even though I was clearly looking at my best friend. She looked even prettier than before. She was literally glowing, and she had the most beautiful grey eyes I ever saw.

She opened her mouth and let out a high-pitched screech that almost burst my eardrums. She reached out and snatched the chain that Ray gave me off my neck. "Your heaven leads you to hell!" She blared before kicking me in the stomach so hard that it knocked me off my feet.

I was waiting for the sand to catch my fall, but it wasn't there. I was falling down a big hole, and it was getting hotter and hotter the further I went down. I woke up and took a sharp breath trying to see what was going on. I looked over at Ray's sexy ass, who was still sleep, and everything came rushing to me. I wasn't dreaming about him and the round-house-special he hit me with last night, but I was dreaming about Adalis. What the fuck was that all about? "Your heaven leads you to hell." I whispered to myself. I looked at Ray and knew exactly what she was getting to. I felt like I was in heaven whenever I was with him. "I guess I'm going to hell, best friend, but I don't care because Ray gone be there with me, so it's all good." I joked before sitting up to get out the bed.

Ray stirred. "What?"

"Nothin', bae, I'm about to go make you some breakfast." I said before leaning down and kissing his lips.

He rolled over. "Make a lot. We 'bout to have company. Feed the dog too."

Later that afternoon, I was in the kitchen with Kamya cleaning up. Ray called his sisters over to eat breakfast and surprised them with me and the puppy. They were both excited about the puppy, but Kamya was the only one excited to see me. Babie was like her brother. Hard to please, and even harder to get along with. The only person I saw her be nice to other than her family was Adalis. They were close as hell, so of course she didn't like the fact that I was here.

"How you get your booty so fat, Jas?" Kamya asked while scrubbing the electric stove off.

I was washing dishes. I looked over at her. "Girl, where that come from?"

"Because your booty wasn't that fat before, now its biggg!" She joked goofily. Kamya was a pretty girl that walked and talked like any other, but her brain wasn't programmed the same. She had a rare disorder that made her slow at learning, maturing, and angering. It gave her a child-like innocence. I loved her so much.

"I just grew up, that's all. My mamma blessed me with a booty." I answered while wiggling my ass, making it shake through the tight pajama pants I had on.

She looked at me in shock. "I can ask my mamma for booty?"

"No, silly!" I said in between laughter. "Why you asking me this though?"

"Because this boy I like at school started going with this big booty girl, so I figured if my booty get big, he'll like me back."

I stopped washing dishes and looked at her sadly. "Girl, fuck that nigga! You ain't gotta change yourself for that nigga, that's his loss. If he don't like you for you, then he ain't the one for you. You perfect, Mya. You hear me?"

She nodded her head sheepishly with those big eyes set on me.

"What y'all in here talkin' about?" Ray asked as he walked into the kitchen with Babie.

"Tellin' Mya some shit she don't need to know, I bet." Babie said before hopping her little evil ass on the counter.

"No, she's not!" Shanay countered urgently. She didn't want to get in trouble. "Jassy was being nice, telling me good stuff."

I looked at Babie with that little smug smirk on her face and thought about slapping it off, but I was smarter than that, so I winked at her and walked up to Ray with a little extra sway in my hips and wrapped my arms around his neck. "Where you goin', bae? Can I come?"

He had on this black Gucci jacket with fur around the collar that looked so sophisticated on him. He looked every bit of the mob-boss they were making him to be. He wrapped his arms around me and rested his hands on the top of my ass. "Got some shit to handle, I'll be back later. You can go to Lenox and pick up the chain I ordered for Buddy though."

I whipped my neck back. "You ordered a chain for the damn dog? Really? You too much."

"He apart of the family, so he get family treatment. Oh, yeah, go get the DG logo on the back of yo' neck too, wit' Rampage up under it. Every Dinero Girl in my camp gotta put they nigga's name under the logo, so don't look at me like that."

I stepped back with a hand on my hip. "You gone get my name too?"

"We'll see." He went in his jacket pocket and pulled out a bankroll. "That's 5,000. The chain gone cost $2,000. Do what you want wit' the rest."

"Okay, bae."

"Take my sisters wit' you. The dog too."

Babie sucked her teeth. "I'm goin' back to mamma house, I don't want to go."

"Well, take Kamya and Buddy. I'll see y'all later."

He kissed us all on the foreheads, then tried to leave, but I stopped him. "How we supposed to get there?"

He stopped and thought about it. Then out of nowhere, an evil smile formed on his face. He pulled out his phone. "Call this number I'm about to text you and tell him I said to bring you there and back. His name is AK."

Malik D. Rice

CHAPTER 4
~ Rampage ~

I was sixteen and probably experienced more things than most men twice my age, but I'd never stepped foot inside of a strip club until now. Magic City was a small but notorious spot that was home to plenty of rappers and dope-boys throughout the city. When Vonte called me and told me to meet him there, I got excited, but I couldn't really show it. Another thing I was being taught about being a made man was not to show too many emotions.

It was only 4:00pm so I knew the place wasn't going to be off-the-chain, but I didn't care. I just wanted to be able to say that I'd been there. I only had Black with me, who was driving the Escalade we came in. Black was twenty years old, and he'd been to plenty of strip clubs in his time, so the experience wasn't the same for him. He was more excited about meeting with Vonte than actually being at the club.

The security staff easily peeped who we were, and what we represented. They didn't bother to ask us for identification or pat us down. We were getting the VIP treatment. "Vonte must done told them we was comin' to meet him or some shit?" I asked Black as we walked inside.

"Nah, just like that club we went to last week, anybody wit' DG get special treatment. Freddy got somethin' goin' on wit' the owners of all the hot spots in the city or some shit."

Freddy was the Capo over the whole city of Atlanta, and the uncle to Vonte and his twin brother, Ronte. Their bloodline was becoming legendary, and I was a part of it.

The place was damn-near empty except for a half-dozen dancers, Vonte, and his entourage. They were throwing loads of dollar bills in the air. "These hoes probably make more money than us."

Black put a hand around my shoulder. "Ain't no probably, nigga. Them hoes most definitely make more than us."

I shook my head disappointedly. Here I was risking my life and taking lives for a living, and all these hoes had to do was shake they asses. I had to tighten up, but I was gone have to address that problem later on. I had to see what the big homie wanted with me.

Vonte was in a VIP section on a sofa texting on one phone with two more in his lap while his entourage entertained themselves with the dancers. We were let inside the section by security. You couldn't be within arm's reach of a made man without his permission, so Black joined Vonte's entourage while I took a seat on the sofa next to him. "Wassup, big bruh?"

He didn't even bother to look my way, he just continued typing away on his iPhone. I was tempted to speak my mind, but this wasn't Kapo I was talking to. Vonte was known to be very bipolar and ruthless. The wrong word could tick him off, just like that, so I just sat back and pulled my own phone out.

"Put that shit down!" He commanded sharply.

"Damn, I can't use my shit?" I was a made man, so I had room for a little back-talk, but I had to keep in mind that this was the nigga that made me a made man, so the situation was tricky. I had to get more familiar with him.

"You about to get Maniac on the line?" He asked while he still typed away without a glance my way.

"Nah."

"I know you not because Maniac on the China bus right now on his way to Delaware."

That caught me by surprise. "How you found him? I been lookin' everywhere for that black-ass-nigga."

"I got my ways."

"Why you sendin' him to Delaware?"

"Because that's the terms that I came to wit' Big Bank, plus

Dilluminati at war wit' some gang out there, but they on the losing end, so I figured they'll need a savage like him out there. Long-story-short, you'll never see Maniac in Atlanta again."

"You ain't have to waste yo' time cleanin' up my mess, big bruh. I swear I had everything under control."

He finally sat his phone down and looked over at me. "I believe you, young nigga. I got my reasons for makin' you a made man; you ain't got shit to prove to me. That wasn't yo' fault, plus I need you to focus on other things."

"Like what?"

He bent down and dug into his already open Hermes bag. He came out with a small envelope and handed it to me.

"What's this?" I held the envelope awkwardly. I knew it wasn't money because it was paper-thin, so I was curious.

He was bobbing his head to the music that the DJ was playing. It was a song from his brother Ronte. It was a new song I'd never heard. He held up his index finger. "This the part right here. Listen!"

Ain't shit changeeee!
Still runnin' wit' dem youngins,
that'll eat ya faceeee!
Nun of my shooter's really scared,
to catch a caseeee!
Youngest mob-boss in the game,
like Rampageeee!
New To The Game!
Young nigga stay the sameeee—

I was so shocked I just sat there with wide eyes and an open mouth that was slowly turning into a goofy smile. I was trying to fight it, but fuck that. One of the hottest rappers in the game just shouted me out on his song. The whole world was about to be screaming my name.

He motioned for one of his boys to come over who kept a watchful eye on us the whole time. He gave him one of his phones and told him to take a picture of us. I looked up at the camera with the meanest look I could muster, and the next thing I knew, the flash from the phone was going off. The picture was taken.

Vonte got his phone back and went to work. "That song drop in two days. I made Ronte put you in that song, and I just posted that picture on my Instagram page wit' you tagged in it. I made you the youngest made man in Dilluminati and changed yo' whole life, young nigga. You owe me, and you gone pay me back by handlin' that business inside that envelope. Open it."

I was so caught up in the hype I had forgotten all about the envelope already. I looked down at the envelope, opened it, and pulled out nine pictures. "What's this all about?"

He took the rubber band out of his hair and let his dreads hang loose. "Them niggas that I need knocked off the map for different reasons. On the back of them pictures is addresses you gone be able to find them at. I don't know when, but they'll be there at least one day out the week."

I shined the light from my phone on the pictures so I could see them better in the dim light. "These the addresses where they lay they heads at?"

"Some houses, some apartments, and some stores. You gotta catch 'em and whack 'em."

"Nine bodies? That's a lot of killin' to be doin' for free."

"Ain't nothin' free, lil' nigga. All I'm sendin' you to do is whack 'em. What you take from the scene is all you. Them ain't no light weights, so you should come out nice. But it's one thing you need to know before I let you off the leash."

I looked at him sideways. "What?"

"You fuck up, you get whacked. You get caught, you get whacked. You in the big leagues now. Ain't no room for mistakes.

Remember that."

***

I was in the back of the Escalade entertaining all my new fans on Instagram. Vonte had just over 200,000 followers, and him posting me on his page made it official, I was famous. Only an hour and some change had past and I already had over 30,000 followers on my page. It was a good thing I took a screenshot of the picture and put it on my page because he had already took the picture down off of his, but I wasn't tripping because I was already in the door. A shout-out on Ronte's song, and 30,000 followers, I would've whacked them niggas for Vonte on the strength. He just made me a living legend.

I was reading my comments, sucking up all the glory when I got a call from Lisa. "Wassup cuzzo? You seen that shit, huh?" I just knew she was calling me to talk about that picture with Vonte.

"Hell yeah, nigga! You all poppin' and shit. I'm so proud of you, cousin, I swear."

"You ain't seen nothin'. Ronte 'bout to drop a song in a few days, and he shouted me out on that muthafucka."

I heard her gasp. "Oh my fuckin' godddd! You better not be lying."

"You know I don't do no cappin', lil' girl. Yo' cousin doin' it big now."

"I'm finna tell everybody'! Oh, yeah. JD gone be on the way back from Miami soon."

That was good news right there. All I could think about was that money I was gone be collecting from Kapo once I whacked his ass. The fact that I was about to take my neices father away from her didn't bother me because I was gone take care of her like my own. And Lisa could always find another nigga to dick her down.

"Aight, cool. Just let me know when he touchdown and remember not to tell him. Kapo want it to be a surprise."

CHAPTER 5
~Toe-Tag ~

I was laid up with Shanay and Lil' Tee watching a rerun of Love and Hip-Hop when Rampage called me and told me it was time to ride. Shanay bitched and moaned, but I wasn't trying to hear it. The streets were calling and I had to pick up. I promised Shanay that I would start picking up for her too and got the fuck on. We had business to be handled in the streets, and I was top lieutenant. I had shots to call.

My first stop was to Monster's apartment he shared with his girlfriend, ZyAsia. She was a pretty light skinned, big body woman with some height on her. Monster was a big nigga and he liked his bitches in the same fashion.

"Wassup, lil' brother? You coming to take my man away from me again?" She asked after she opened the door.

"Yeah, you know how this shit be. I promise I'll bring him back in one piece." I walked past her into the apartment.

"You better. Monster! Tee here for you!" She yelled before walking to the back to get him.

"Tee? Heyyyy, baby daddy!" KyAsia's little sister, Missy, said as she rushed into the living room.

I shook my head and prepared myself for the usual harassment. She been trying to get some of this dick since she laid eyes on a nigga last year. She was a mini version of her big sister. She wasn't ugly or anything, she just wasn't mini enough for me. "My baby mamma in D-building, apartment 2C. I don't know what you talkin' 'bout."

She came and invited herself to a seat next to me. "Boy, you need to stop fighting this shit. A young boss nigga like you need a boss bitch like me to hold you down." She put a hand on my lap.

I slapped it off and stood up. "Nah, I'm straight, baby girl."

"One hit of this pussy and yo' lil' young ass gone be gone nigga!"

She tried to pull me down on top of her, but I snatched away from her, and pulled my gun out. "Keep touching me and I'm gone pop yo' big ass one of these days. I done told you 100 times I don't want you, shawty. I'm straight on you!"

"Missy, why the hell you keep fuckin' wit' that crazy ass nigga? His name ain't Toe-Tag for nothing." Said Monster as he walked into the living room while zipping up his jacket with a stupid ass smile on his face.

"What the fuck so funny, nigga?"

He put his hands up. "I ain't the one trying to rape you, my nigga. Wassup though? Where we goin'?"

I looked at Missy on the couch, and ZyAsia in the kitchen. "I'ma tell you in the car. We ain't got too much time." I knew a nigga who knew a nigga that came to tow my car this morning and was going to fix it for a good price, so we were riding in Monster's black 2011 Nissan Maxima. Unlike my car, it was low-key and could blend in easily. The perfect car for the job.

"So, what's the job, young nigga?" He asked as he bent a corner onto Moreland Avenue.

"You know Rampage just went to go meet with Vonte. He just texted me a address and told me to meet him there."

He glanced at me. "What you think this all about? One thing I done learned about that young nigga Vonte is he about his business. Money and murder. It got something to do with one of 'em."

I nodded my head in agreement. "Hopefully both."

"That's the truck right there." I said pointing out the Escalade in the parking lot of the Varsity restaurant.

Monster parked as closed to the truck as possible. "I wonder why he told us to meet him out here."

I opened the door, put my feet on the ground, and pulled my

hood over my head. "Let's go see."

We got out of the car, walked over to the truck, and got in the back with Rampage. He was sitting all the way in the back glued to his phone with a Chuck E. Cheese smile on his face. "Nigga get a lil' fame and don't know how to act." I joked.

I couldn't be mad at my nigga. Just like the money, fame for him was fame for me. I got 6,000 new followers since Vonte shouted him out. I was all on his page.

He looked up at me with an evil smirk. "I'm lovin' this shit, bruh." He typed something else, then put it down. "Look tho'. On some real shit, we got a lot of work to put in." He brought us up to speed on everything from Maniac's whereabouts, to the jobs that Vonte expected us to do.

"That's a lot of bodies right there. How much he paying?" Monster stated then asked. He been doing this shit for a minute, and we still came to him for guidance and advice. No matter how many stripes me or Rampage had, he would always be a big homie to us.

"Well it ain't really no set price like the Kapo job. He said whatever we get off the targets we can keep, so I guess that's gone have to do." Rampage informed matter-of-factly.

Monster looked back at him sideways. "Gone have to do? Nigga, that ain't gone do. Murder is a business. We kill for cash, not for fame, nigga. What you trying to call a payment is really a bonus. When you do business with somebody talking about killing, you *always* get a ticket on each body. Bonuses ain't promised. Why should he get a guaranteed body if we can't get a guaranteed paycheck?"

Rampage shrugged his shoulders. "What? You want me to call him up and tell him I ain't gone do it unless he put a ticket on the bodies?"

"Nah, it's too late. The deal already sealed, can't go back from that. We gone handle the business, but after it's all said and done, you need to let him know that we gone need a ticket on each body from now on. You got a whole camp to feed, nigga, you can't be making deals like that."

Rampage nodded his head in understanding, and I sat back in my seat staring into space thinking on Monster's words. Our whole camp was mostly known for our ruthlessness and gunplay, but it just really settled in that we were real-life hitmen.

I turned around in my seat and looked back at Rampage. "Who we gone hit first?"

He picked a handful of pictures up off the seat next to him and started thumbing through them. "This address right there is for a nigga that go by the name of Solo in Stone Mountain."

For some reason that name was familiar to me. "Solo from Stone Mountain? You talkin' about the nigga that's over that Plugg Rich shit out there?"

"I guess so, my nigga. I don't really give a fuck though. A nigga name on this list, his ass gone."

"I wonder why Vonte want Solo head."

"He told me some of these niggas refused to fall up under Dilluminati, so they gotta go. He want they turf and they numbers. I don't know which ones, and he never said nothing about the other ones."

"Make sense, that's how the game goes. If Strong refuse our request, his ass gone have to go too. Folks gone learn about bucking on this DG shit." Monster said matter-of-factly.

"Y'all niggas already followed through on that?" Asked Rampage.

"Hell yeah, that's where we was coming from when them niggas caught us slippin' at the gas station." I answered.

Rampage nodded his head. "We'll handle him somewhere along the line, but right now I need one of y'all to call G-Baby and tell him to round up a few shooters. We going hunting tonight."

Malik D. Rice

CHAPTER 6
~ Rampage ~

I was still in the back of the Escalade watching the movie Blue Hill Avenue on my iPad. I still had Black in the driver's seat watching our surroundings while Toe-Tag handled the business inside. The address for Solo was an ordinary suburban house in a somewhat classy neighborhood. Anyone would open the door for a female stranger before they would open it for a male one, so we had one of the Dinero Girls ring the doorbell to get it open, and the rest was easy.

"There they go." Said Black.

I looked up and saw a few of the Young Mobsters escorting a woman and two kids out of the back door toward the other Escalade that was parked in the backyard beside mine. "Stay in the truck." I climbed out and walked toward them.

Toe-Tag walked up to me. "The house clear. That's his baby mamma right there, and the baby she holding is Solo's. The other one she had wit' another nigga before they met." He informed while smoking a cigarette.

"Aight, cool." I waved my hand in front of my face to clear the foul smell of the smoke he was blowing. "What you tell her? You ain't have to threaten her? Slap her? Nothing? She just walked up out that bitch willingly?"

He shrugged his shoulders. "When we went in there, she ain't scream or nothin'. The bitch wasn't even scared. She just stared us down and asked what we wanted calmly."

"And what you tell her?"

"First, I told her I need her to show me the stash. She did it. Then, I told her I need her to come wit' me. She packed three bags, and there she go." He pointed at the Escalade.

"What was in the stash?"

"Some money and a few chains. Nothin' serious."

"Hold the chains for me. Do what you want with the money."

"Where you goin'?"

I pointed at the truck. "About to go talk to lil' shawty."

I made the Mobsters clear out the truck and wait outside. I opened the door and climbed in. I cut on the overhead light so I could see her better in the dark. They were sitting all the way in the back, so I had to sit sideways in one of the single seats to see them.

She stared me down. "What do you want?" She asked calmly just like Toe-Tag described. She was an older black lady, probably in her early forties. She looked good for her age, but it was something about those beady eyes of hers that told it all. I been around enough pain and suffering in my life to know a scarred soul when I saw one. The little girl even looked like she'd been through some shit, and she couldn't be any older than ten or eleven.

"First off, I just want you to know I'm not here to hurt you or yo' kids."

She shrugged her shoulders nonchalantly. "Believe me, honey. You'll be doing us a big favor. The afterlife couldn't possibly be any worse than the one we're cursed with now." She retorted matter-of-factly.

I raised an eyebrow. That wasn't the response I was expecting. "You serious too, ain't you?"

"As a heart attack. Now, if you're not here for me or my kids, I'm going to take it you're here for my baby's father."

"Yeah, I'm here for Solo."

She looked down at her oldest daughter. "Cover your ears, lil' girl." She waited for the girl to do that, then leaned in closer to me. "This is the thing. Solo is probably the foulest man I've ever been with. He abuses me and my daughter, physically, mentally, and sexually. You know why I stay? Because my ass don't got nowhere to go, or nobody to go to, so I've been allowing all this shit to go on for *years*! Not to mention the fact that he'll find and kill us if I ever tried to leave." She spat with heavy emotion.

"I thought you didn't care about dying."

She shook her head. "It's complicated. I don't care about dying, but I don't want it to be by his hands. If that makes any sense to you."

"No, it don't. But my opinion don't matter. The only thing that matters right now is if you gone set the nigga up for me."

"I can tell you where he's at right now, but I need something from you in return."

I sighed. "What you want?"

"I just need $2,000 so I can get out of town and start over. That should hold me until I find a job."

"That ain't shit. Now, where Solo at?"

"I need something else."

"You pushing it. I could just wait for the nigga to come back and don't got to give you shit."

"You could do that, but you'll never know where his stash house is because he'll die a slow death before he give you his life savings."

"You better not be lying to me, shawty What else you need?"

"I need you to promise me that you'll take care of my daughter." She looked down at the little sleeping beauty in her arms. "I love this little girl with all my heart, but every time I look at her face I think about her daddy and I can't live life hating my own daughter. I know Solo got at least $500,000 in his stash, and that's not even including the drugs. I just need you to take care of my baby, please."

This lady was fucked up in the head, but for a half-ticket, I would've took care of both of the brats. "Aite, I'll do it. Now, where the nigga at?"

"Swear on what you stand on that you'll forever take care of my baby girl."

"Man, I ain't got time for all this shit. I just said I'll do it."

She shook her head frantically. "No! You have to swear, or you can just kill all three of us now!"

I took a deep breath and looked at the little girl in her arms. She was probably nine or ten months. No older than a year old. "Fuck it. On Dilluminati I'll take care of lil' shawty."

"Thank you. Her name is Karma."

***

I looked down at the little girl looking up at me. "What you lookin' at, lil girl?" She started laughing, trying to grab at my face with her little hands.

"Dawg. We killers, not babysitters. What the fuck was you thinkin'?" Toe-Tag asked me angrily.

"I was thinkin' I want what that nigga got in that stash spot."

"If you want the stash, you torture that hoe until she tell you where it's at. We don't bargain with no muthafuckin' victims. Fuck wrong with you?" He was sitting all the way in the back next to me, looking down at the baby in disgust.

Monster nodded his head. "He's right, Rampage, but guess what? It's already done. He took the baby, and the hoe gave us both of the locations we needed."

"Aight. If she already gave us what we want, then why you still got the lil' baby in yo' hands?"

"Because I put it on DG I was gone make sure lil' shawty straight, and that's what I'm gone do, nigga. Anything else you need me to explain, big dawg?" I asked sarcastically.

He took a deep breath and paused for a few seconds to calm himself down. "Look bro', I ain't trying to argue with you. All I'm saying is that you got to watch what you do. You know why?

Because you got all these folks looking up to you now. So, if you do some shit, they gone think it's cool. And what you did tonight wasn't cool. We can't be known for the niggas that be bargaining with the victims. That ain't no good look in our line of work."

At the time I wasn't thinking about it like that. Even though I had some experience in the game, it didn't stop the fact that I was still new to it. Whether I liked it or not, I had a long way to go before I could be able to carry the full weight of a made man on my shoulders by myself. That's why I was glad I had my niggas. "Like Monster said, that shit already done, but I most definitely won't slip up like that again, bruh."

"Good. I got a idea too." Said Toe-Tag.

"Talk to me."

"Instead of dropping the baby off, let's bring her with us to handle the business."

I looked at him confusingly. "You want to bring a one-year old lil' girl with us to whack her daddy?''

"Think about it, bruh. We can probably make the nigga kill himself if we got his daughter and he think we gone do somethin' to her. Make our job easier, plus the police ain't gone investigate no suicide for real."

"Yeah, that sound about right. You keep thinkin' like that you gone end up takin' my spot." I joked seriously.

He waved me off dismissively. "I don't want yo' spot, bruh. The throne is yours. Just don't never forget the niggas that was right here when you needed 'em."

"You been knowin' me all yo' life, Tee. You already know how I'm comin'. You and everybody else in our camp. Loyalty 4 Eva." I promised.

Monster slapped the clip into his AR-14. "Let's go whack this fuck nigga. We got a long list to cross out. Drive this muthafucka, Black!"

"Say less." Black crunk up and pulled off with the other Escalade trailing close behind.

CHAPTER 7
~ Jasmine ~

I was in a deep sleep when I heard music playing from a phone and felt someone's hand on my ass. "Hey, baby." I whispered in a sleepy voice. Rampage was sitting on the bed looking down at me. The sun was coming up and he still had on the same clothes from yesterday. "What time is it?"

"It's 6:30. Get yo' ass up, it's Christmas. I got a present for you." He said before getting up and walking out of the room.

I got up, went to the bathroom, brushed my teeth, then made my way to the living room where all the commotion was at. Music was playing, weed smoke was in the air, and everybody was joking and laughing. I walked in the living room and stopped dead in my tracks when I looked down at all the money on the coffee table.

"We got blood on that money, and we *still* count it!" Ramage song along to Future's song while sitting in a chair that was scooted up to the table counting a large bankroll just like Toe-Tag and Monster.

I caught my breath and tried to act normal, like I was used to seeing hundreds of thousands of dollars in cash on the regular. I walked further into the living room and sat on Rampage's lap. "Good morning y'all!" I said over the music so they could hear me.

They nodded at me, and Rampage pulled me in for a kiss. "Wassup, pretty bitch of mine?"

"Ummm, I don't know. You tell me. Where my present at?" I asked with my sweetest smile, looking down at the bankroll in his hand.

He slapped me on the head with the money. "You got yo' eyes on the wrong prize." He pointed at the two little kids on the floor playing with Buddy.

I recognized the little boy, that was Toe-Tag's son, but I never saw the little girl. She was pretty though. "What the hell you pointing at them for?" I asked with a blank expression plastered on my face.

"You see that lil' girl right there? Her name is Karma and she yours. You gone take care of her like she yo' own daughter. Understand me?"

This nigga had to be bullshitting. "That's a human being, not a kitten. What you mean she mine? I ain't push her out. Where you get her from? How you just gone volunteer me to take care of somebody else child?"

"If this right here gone work between us, you gone have to learn how to follow directions without questions. I don't care if I come in this muthafucka with a baby tiger and tell you to take care of it, you need to do it. Without question. You supposed to trust yo' nigga and respect him enough not to question his judgement."

I looked back down at the cute little bundle of responsibility. She was cute as hell and I always wanted a baby, but this wasn't my baby. "Okay, daddy. I'll do it."

He handed me one of the bundles of money from his pile on the table. "Here. That's $10,000 right there. Do what you want with it, it's yours, bae."

"Thanks." I said dryly.

"What? You don't want the money?" He asked trying to take it back.

I snatched my hand away from him. "Of course, I want the money, Ray. I want a real baby too."

"That is a real baby." He retorted slyly.

I slapped him on the head with the stack of money. "You know what I mean, nigga."

"Just chill, we'll get there eventually. Just take care of this one for now. Can you do that for daddy?"

I poked my lip out and nodded my head sheepishly. I couldn't bring myself to tell this nigga no.

"That's my bitch." He kissed me on my forehead and stood up.

I was on his lap so I had to stand up with him. "Where you going now? You just came in. You ain't even change. Go take a shower and change. By the time you get out I'll have breakfast ready for you."

He shook his head. "No time for all that, I got places to be. Just take care of the kids and the dog."

I put a hand on my hip. "I gotta watch Lil' Tee too?"

"Yeah. Shanay gone be here soon to pick him up, just chill." Toe-Tag answered while stuffing his pile of money into a small duffle bag.

Rampage kissed me, the two kids, and the dog, on the forehead and they were gone.

Later that afternoon, I was in the living room staring at the money that Rampage left on the table. I already took plenty of pictures with it that I planned to post on Instagram but put *ever* dollar back even though I heard Rampage say he didn't have time to get finish counting it. Test or no test, I never been a thief and didn't plan on starting now.

I looked at the kids and the dog sleeping comfortably on a pallet I made for them on the floor. I let them play all morning, fed them, and put a dab of NyQuil in their milks. I had to get my head right; my life was changing fast. Rampage wasn't playing about taking me to another world.

I heard somebody knocking on the door and went to answer it. It was Shanay. "Hey. Come in. He sleeping right over here."

Before she could make it to her son, she stopped in her tracks and looked at the money on the table. "Tee just dropped a duffle bag off on me and left right back out the house. You know what they been up to? I be so worried for they stupid asses."

I sat back down on the couch and shrugged my shoulders. "I

have no clue, girl. I'm new to this world. I'm still trying to figure out what the hell I done got myself into."

She came and sat next to me. "I ain't got all the answers, but I can tell you this, lil' mamma. Them boys we was fuckin' with ain't boys no more. Them some grown ass men, doing grown man shit now. As you can see, they getting grown man money too."

"I'm with you, girl. I'm worried about 'em. All I want is to live a happy life with Ray."

She started chuckling while shaking her head.

"What's so funny?"

"I always knew you and Rampage was fucking. I tried to make Tee tell me, but he more loyal to Rampage than his own fuckin' son."

I cut my eyes at her. "So, you think I ain't shit like everybody else, huh?"

"I mean, of course you was wrong for fucking your best friend's nigga behind her back, but at the same time you ain't perfect, and I damn sure ain't either. Who am I to judge? I was just laughing because my suspicions was right all along."

"I think Adalis haunting me. I had a dream about her."

She put a hand on my thigh. "Nah, she ain't haunting you, baby. It's called a guilty conscience."

"You really cool as hell. I always thought you was mean."

"I ain't gone lie. I just used to act like that because I thought you was fuckin' my nigga too."

"Not even. Believe it or not, Rampage is the only nigga I let hit this shit."

She looked at me with an evil smile. "Oh, he done hit you with the round-house-special, huh?"

"Yassssss, bitch!" I said with my tongue out. "He hit me with it before Adalis."

She started laughing so hard she woke up the kids. "You a slime hoe, but I like you. Plus, our niggas close as hell. Might as well start kicking it."

I was glad she said that because Adalis was basically my only real friend, and ever since she died, I really been rocking solo. "What you about to get into? I be so damn bored cooped up in this damn house."

"The Dinero Girls about to have a lil' meeting, and they want me to come, but I ain't really feelin' them hoes like that. They ain't nothing but a bunch of groupies on a come-up-mission." She got up and picked up her son.

I went to go get my new daughter. "You mean the girls from the neighborhood?"

"Nah, hoes from the neighborhood ain't really got no choice but to fall in suit, but they the minority. It's mostly hoes from other places these niggas be saving and stamping."

"So, what they be bringing to the table?"

"They sell they souls for money and fame. They do *whatever* the niggas say."

Malik D. Rice

CHAPTER 8
~ Kapo ~

So much for my retirement plan. I had blessings from my nigga, Freddy, to retire in four years. I had already begun planning out my future as a successful car dealership owner. I wanted to open a chain of luxury dealerships and run them myself, but that wasn't possible now. I would still be able to own them, but with the new promotion I got, running even one of them would be completely impossible.

The original Godfather of Dilluminati in Georgia was a man named,Drop Top. He was the uncle of Dinero. The nigga that started Dilluminati. I guess he thought that would save him from the consequences of breaking DG law. He wanted to lay low from the heat of the feds, but his request was denied. A few days later, his body was found naked, floating far in the Pacific Ocean with *4 Eva* carved into his forehead. Now Masio was the new Godfather in Georgia, and he took it upon himself to bump me up from a Don to the muthafucking Pope. The promotion was mandatory and non-negotiable which is why I called this meeting with Masio and Freddy. We were in a famous five-star restaurant downtown called Bizzy's. They catered to the city's most Elite, and we were dining in the VIP section of that restaurant where a cup of water cost $150. We were above the majority of the minority. We had a private booth that was guarded by a sparkling gold curtain, and a few of our guards right outside of that.

"Why you ain't order nothin'?" Asked Masio after the waitress walked off with her assistant.

"Because I don't got no money to be splurging like that. I invest mine, not throw it away." I answered.

Freddy cleared his throat. "In other words, he trying to tell you he's cheap as fuck!" He stated jokingly, laughing at his own joke.

I sat there with a straight face while they both laughed at me. "Y'all done?"

"You know I gotta fuck with you, bro'. Wassup though? Why you call the meeting?" Asked a more serious Freddy.

I looked at him dead in the eyes. "I thought we had an agreement as far as my retirement was concerned."

"We did, and I told Masio that, but he insisted on makin' you the Pope."

I turned from Freddy and looked over at Masio. He was a big black intimidating figure, but that was in a physical sense. The wars of made men were mostly mental. By interfering with my retirement, he was unofficially sparking a mental war between us. His goal to keep me in the game for whatever reasons, and my goal to get out of the game for obvious reasons. "This is the part where you explain to me why."

The waitresses came back with the drinks and promised the food would be following shortly. He took a sip of the mixed drink he'd ordered and returned eye contact. "I made you Pope because you're the most qualified person for the position. Point-blank-period."

"What's wrong with Freddy's antennas? Y'all niggas thicker than cold gravy. Why not give the position to him?"

He cut his eyes at Freddy, then back at me. "Freddy got his hands full with Atlanta as it is. You gone be able to handle Georgia wit' no problem. I ain't want to be Godfather, but I ain't have no choice. I sucked it up because I know that's how the game goes; you need to do the same."

I loved my hood, and I loved Dilluminati, but I loved my soul more. There was no way I could ever be at peace with myself as long as I remained an active leader in Dilluminati. When you called shots in our organization, majority of them just so happened to be shots into someone's head. I never killed anyone, but I ordered the deaths of more than a few people, and that was just was a Don over one-quarter of a city. I could only imagine the things I'd have to make sure got done as a Pope over an entire state. I was tired of it all.

"Let me guess. While I'm running Georgia smoothly, what you gone be doing?"

"Making sure you running Georgia smoothly. I ain't like Drop Top. I'm not with all the extracurricular activities. I only got one person to worry about, and that's you."

The waitresses came back with the food. They apologized for the wait and left. The curtain slid back closed on its own. They dug into their seafood while I got my thoughts together.

At the moment I was angry and indecisive. That wasn't a good mix. When you're emotional, the chances are very high that you'll say something you'll regret in the future. Fortunately, my brain still knew how to work when my heart was trying to take over.

I took a healthy breath. "I can't say I'm happy about your decision, but I know what I signed up for. If Dilluminati needs me, I'll be there because Dilluminati was there when I was in need. Sometimes you may not know the reason, but I am a believer that everything happens for a reason."

"Nigga, you gone be like the next Malcolm X of Dilluminati or some shit. If you don't do nothin' else, you gone talk that shit." Freddy joked with a mouth full of lobster meat.

Here I was being robbed of a peaceful future, and they were laughing like shit was funny. As they sat there and laughed at the joke, I smiled inwardly. They were too caught up in the matrix to even be playing these types of games with me. Little did they know, the only reason I kept running away from the power they kept trying to give me is because I know what kind of monster I would turn into with it, but they were asking for this shit, so now they had it coming.

Malik D. Rice

CHAPTER 9
~ Rampage ~

Five long days had passed since that meeting with Vonte, and a lot of blood had been shed in his name. Blood that was on our hands, but we really didn't give a fuck because we were getting rich in the process. The more money, fame and glory I got, the more invincible I felt. Fuck what Kapo was talking about; the deeper I got in the game, the better I felt. I don't understand how he could possibly see this blessing as a curse. The nigga had to be blind.

We had three more targets left on the list, and I had a master plan to eliminate all three with one stone. With one nigga to be exact. His name was Xavier. He was an explosives dealer from Seattle, but he moved to Cobb County when he got too hot up there. Little did he know, his ass was hot all over again, but the only difference was that he wasn't gone run from this heat.

The address Vonte gave me was to a barber shop in midtown. I had some of the Young Mobsters lay on that muthafucka every day until they spotted the fat ass nigga. I did my homework on him and he had a helluva operation and was known to run with a pack of ruthless wolves that were extra loyal to him. No wonder why he didn't get with Dilluminati, he didn't have to. He gone wish he would've when I get finished with his ass. Just had to get a hold of him first.

"So, this nigga stay in a castle in the middle of nowhere that he barely come out of, and when he do, he got a pack of highly trained killers with him? Either Vonte got us on a suicide mission, or he really got that much faith in us." Said Monster.

We were in a VIP room on the second floor of a club in East Atlanta Village called KINKY that we took over. The crowd used to be mostly white, now shit was different. Ronte rented the place out for a mixtape release party just under two months ago, and the rest was history. It was basically a new kick it spot for DG now. We practically owned the place. Well, we practically owned the owner.

I was looking down at the crowd from the mirrored window in the room. The place was jumping for a Thursday night. "I doubt he got us on a suicide mission, so I take it he got that much faith in us. And his faith in the right place because I got a plan to solve our last three problems with one solution."

"I got to hear this one." Said Black.

I waved him off. "Just chill. You can't rush perfection."

"We need to hurry up and get this shit over with because we got too much other shit going on." Monster stated.

"I understand that, big bro', but look at our line of work. We gone always have too much goin' on."

"As long as the money adding up I can't even trip."

"Look at us, nigga. We living like rock stars. Designer clothes, diamonds on our necks and wrists, guns galore. The money most definitely adding up."

Quay took a swig of champagne straight out the bottle. "I ain't complaining at all. I got a big bag in my safe. I'm living the best life I ever lived."

"And it's gone continue to be that way. Niggas just got to keep putting in work." I said.

"Speaking of putting in work. Where the hell Toe-Tag been at lately? That nigga been missing in action for the last two days. Wassup with that?" Asked Quay.

"Toe-Tag been handling other shit. We 'bout to go meet up with him after we leave here."

"That's wassup. What you think about yo' boy AK?" Asked Black while motioning down at the stage where AK was performing his song. The crowd seemed to like him.

"I mean, his music straight. Ain't know the nigga had it in him.

I hope he get signed so he can hit the road and I ain't got to see his ass no more."

We left the club the same way we came in, through the back. Our trucks were waiting for us in the parking lot, but they weren't alone. Two detectives leaned on each of the trucks looking dead at us. "If it ain't the clean-up-crew. How you fellas doing on this fine evening?"

"Nah, y'all the real clean-up crew. Come from a long line of nigga-killers, ain't that right, Superman?" I asked the tallest one leaning on my truck. He looked like Clark Kent, so we started calling him Superman. We had nicknames for all the known officers in our district.

"Watch it, Raylo." Robo Cop warned with a finger pointed at me.

"Y'all niggas been missing in action. Wasssup with that? Y'all don't pull up in the hood harassing niggas no more or nothing." I stated. We had stopped and was standing a few feet away from the officers, and our trucks. It was a standoff.

"Y'all don't be in the *hood* like that anymore, plus, we've been assisting the feds in bringing y'all street-punks down."

I took a few steps closer, and my niggas were right behind me. "How about you watch yo' muthafuckin' mouth, Cracker. Shit done changed around here. I ain't the same nigga you used to chase around the hood. I'll get y'all niggas touched."

Robo Cop took a step closer, and he was face-to-face with me. "You threatening the life of an officer?"

"Nah, I'm promising the death of an officer, and probably the family too."

He swung on me, but I side-stepped it and pushed him back far enough to give me time to pull my Glock off my hip. I didn't even have to turn around to know that my niggas already had their guns out. "Two guns against four. How y'all wanna play this? 'Cause we really don't give no fucks."

Robo Cop looked like he really wanted to try this shit, but I guess Superman was convinced that we would really blow their tops off right here because he lowered his gun and started pulling Robo Cop away.

"You can tell the feds the same thing! They can get it too!" I yelled at them as they walked off.

Monster put a hand over my shoulder and pulled me in close. "Calm down, young nigga."

"Nah, them fuck-niggas came fuckin' with us, bruh! They got me fucked up!"

We all got in the trucks and sped off in the opposite direction as the detectives. "That's they job to harass us, lil' bruh. You can't go around threatening and drawing down on police. We connected, but I don't think all the connections in the world gone save us from whackin' two detectives. We ain't even got the money to be fighting those kinds of cases yet." Monster said once we were deep in the backstreets by Sky Haven Elementary School.

I was mad and wasn't trying to hear shit Monster was talking about. "Fuck all that, bro'. They better stay out my muthafuckin' way, I know that much."

He sighed heavily. "You want me to drop you off at the spot? You need to kick back, lil' bruh. You been in the field too much lately."

I had to think about it. I have been doing a lot of ripping and running lately. It probably was time for me to sit back for a while. "What you gone do? You been running just as much as me."

He glanced back at me through the rearview mirror. "I'm gone spend a night in my own bed and get me some pussy, nigga. What you think?"

"What about Black and Quay?"

"Shit, that's up to you. You the boss. What you want 'em to

do?"

I picked up my Trac Phone and called Black. "I'm 'bout to text you the address where Toe-Tag at. Me and Monster about to take it in for the night. Report back to Monster if y'all need something." Then I hung up.

"That nigga Toe-Tag need to take a break his damn self," Monster said while running a red light on Bouldercrest Rd.

"Nah, I need him in the field. He gone get shit done how it need to be done."

"He got a family at home."

I shrugged my shoulders while texting Black the address. "I know that, and he definitely know that. He just don't give a fuck, so why should I? He want to put in extra work, be my guest."

Malik D. Rice

CHAPTER 10
~ Toe-Tag ~

"What you doing?" Shanay asked me over the phone. I kept my promise and started answering her calls and texts, so she wouldn't trip as much about me not being around.

"I'm handling a lil' business right now. Nothing serious."

"Why do I hear somebody screaming in the background? Sound like a bitch, Tee!" She pointed out angrily.

I started laughing so hard that I almost shit on myself.

"Oh, you think that shit funny, nigga? Bye!"

"Nah! Wait, man! That ain't no bitch, it's a nigga. The youngins workin' on him right now."

"Working on him? What?"

"Goddamn! You gone get a nigga jammed up on this phone, shawty. The nigga getting tortured, man."

"You must think I'm Boo-Boo the Fool!"

I took the phone from my ear and clicked FaceTime so we could see each other on video chat. "You want to see?"

"No. I believe you." She answered in a pouty voice with her head hung low.

"Then why you looking like that?"

"Because I miss you, and Lil' Tee keep asking about you too."

"Look. It's a whole lot goin' on right now. As soon as I can take a break I'm gone pull up."

"Rampage at home with Jasmine right now. Why you can't be at home with me?"

I took a deep breath. This girl knew how to get on a nigga nerves. "Rampage is a Don, bae. That nigga ain't got to leave that apartment at all if he don't want to, but he got so much love for this shit, he still be in the field."

"You got so much love for that shit that you never leave the fuckin' field. I only seen you one time in five days. Like what the fuck?"

"I ain't about to do this with you right now."

"Fuck you!" She spat before hanging up.

I looked at the door of the room where the screaming was coming from and tossed my phone at it so hard that it penetrated the wood before falling to the floor. It was a $10 burnout phone, so I didn't give a fuck about it.

G-Baby and two more Mobsters rushed to the door. "What the fuck goin' on, bruh?"

"Nothing. Them niggas ain't talking yet?"

G-Baby shook his head. "That nigga JD was about to say somethin' but this nigga, Lingo, gone knock the nigga out, and when he got back up, he asked us where he was. I think he got amnesia or some shit."

"Oh, yeah?" I got up out the chair I was sitting in and made my way into the torture room. JD was tied up, laying on the floor in his own blood next to his father who looked like he was taking his last breaths. One in a coma, and the other with so called amnesia. "Fuck it." I had intentions of cutting JD's dick off to spark his memory, for what though? So, he could tell me who else was involved in the robbery? I was starting to think that it was just them. If not, oh well. Rampage was just gone have to settle for $20,000 for them because this was starting to feel like a waste of time. "Y'all whack 'em but make it quiet. These apartments might be abandoned, but you can't forget the ones right next to it."

"How you want it done?" Asked Lingo. He seemed nervous. He was a shooter, not an up-close and personal killer. In fact, all of them seemed nervous.

"Let me find out y'all niggas scared to get up close with it." I walked to the corner of the room, grabbed the sludge hammer, and smashed both of their heads in with two swings each. Then I went back and gave them one more hit a piece just to make sure. Blood and brains were everywhere. "Let's ride, we got shit to do." I dropped the hammer and walked toward the door.

"Who gone clean this shit up?" G-Baby asked while looking at the bodies with wide eyes.

"Nobody. Get the gasoline in the kitchen. We gone burn this bitch down. They need to build some more apartments anyway."

We ended up at the McDonald's down the road from the burning apartments on Cleveland Avenue. We heard sirens in the distance and all. We were inside the restaurant eating when Black walked in with Quay on his heels. I told them to meet me here.

"Wassup, bruh? Why you ain't been around lately?" He asked as he sat at the table with me.

"By around, you mean why I ain't been all up on Rampage? Because I don't got to be. I make my own moves."

He put his hands in the air. "I don't want no smoke, man. The only reason we even here is because Rampage told us to come check up on you."

"All he had to do was call a nigga."

"You know he don't like talking on phones like that. The feds want that nigga head bad. We just drew down on Super Man and Robo Cop in the parking lot behind KINKY."

My mouth dropped and turned into a big smile. "Ain't no wayyyyy! Y'all niggas wild, shawty! Why the fuck y'all do that?"

"Robo Cop swung on Rampage, he side-stepped that shit, then whipped out. It was a stand-off after that."

"I'm surprised y'all ain't have to whack 'em."

"We probably would've if Super Man ain't pull Robo Cop back and tell him to let it go."

I shook my head. "We got to watch our backs. Them two niggas the wrong enemies to be having."

"Fuck them. They said they was investigating with the feds to bring us down. That's who we need to be worrying about."

"Who in Dilluminati ain't getting investigated by the feds these days? They just trying to scare a nigga into slippin' up. Y'all trying to make this run with me?"

"We ain't got no choice, nigga. You in charge when Rampage ain't around."

I smiled sarcastically. "Oh, my bad. I forgot all about that."

I guess Strong felt like he'd have an advantage over me if we met on his turf, but he was wrong. I would always have the advantage over him. I was the predator, and he was the prey. He wanted to meet in the same apartments that we robbed his workers in. I laughed out loud. "This nigga trying to be funny."

"Why you say that?" Lingo asked.

"Because they in the same spot where we robbed the niggas at. It was a fat nigga named Fluffy that looked just like you too." I joked, making G-Baby and the other two Mobsters in the truck start laughing.

"You got me fucked up."

"Watch this, you gone see."

It was almost five in the morning, so nobody else was outside. It was cold as a muthafucka too. "You couldn't find a warmer place to meet at? It's cold as fuck out here, shawty." I said as me and mine approached him and his.

Strong was a muscle-bound nigga that used to play football until a bullet to the leg stopped his career. He been in the streets getting money ever since.

He looked around. "It wasn't nothing wrong with this spot when you robbed my workers. What's wrong with it now?"

"Whose fault is it that they was slipping? Mine or yours?"

"What you want, man? We ain't fucking with nobody. We just trying to get our money and stay out the way."

I buttoned my Hermes trench coat up, put the hood on from my sweater, and pulled the face mask from around my neck onto my face. I looked like Dark Vador with all this black on. It was quickly becoming my favorite color. "I understand all that, but you know how the game go. Sometimes a nigga might get in yo' lane, and if you can't beat 'em, you gotta join 'em."

He looked like he wanted to puff his chest out and say some shit he was gone regret later, but I guess he was smarter than that because it never came out. He knew who he was dealing with. "So, that's what this was all about? Extortion?"

"Don't look at it like extortion. Just look at it like you paying us for our services."

"What services?"

"You went to college and all, but I see that don't make you smart. Just know that if you step up under our umbrella, you ain't got to worry about your workers getting robbed. But if you don't? Just put it like this, you ain't gone be shielded from the harsh weather that's gone come. And it's gone come."

He took a deep breath. "How the hell am I supposed to go to sleep at night knowing I'm being extorted? That's crazy."

I shrugged. "It'll be easier than going to sleep knowing that everything you built is in jeopardy. Don't let your pride be your downfall, my nigga. If it make you feel any better, we getting extorted by the Dons, the Dons getting extorted by the Underbosses, the Underbosses getting extorted by the Capos, the Capos getting extorted by the Pope, the Pope getting extorted by the Godfathers, the Godfathers getting extorted by Dinero, Dinero getting extorted by the Cartel, the Cartel getting extorted by the Government, and the Government getting extorted by the Federal Reserve. The world is built on extortion. Now-a-days, it's like buying insurance on a business. That's how you need to look at it."

Surprisingly a smile crept onto his face. Not a sneer, but a real genuine smile.

"What's so funny?" I asked curiously with a raised brow.

"You got a way with words, young nigga. If you can make a nigga feel good about getting extorted, you can do anything in this world of ours. You set up the next meeting on your terms and we'll discuss payment then." He walked up to me and we shook hands.

"Just like he said, you gone go far in this shit, lil' bro'." Quay told me as we made our way back to the trucks.

I didn't reply, I just sucked it all in. If that's where fate took me, then so be it, but I wasn't fucked up about it. I was content with my current position. Whether I became a made man or not, it didn't matter because I was gone make millions regardless. I was already twenty-five percent closer to my first million, and I was still new to the game.

I'd been up for the better part of two days. By the time I made it to my hotel room on Boulevard Avenue, it was damn-near 6:00am. The sun was up and the birds were chirping. I took a shower, changed my clothes, and collapsed on the bed. The four Mobsters I had with me took turns sleeping. Somebody had to be up on security at all times.

By the time I woke up it was 5:00pm, and I felt more tired than I was when I actually went to sleep. I leaned up and looked around the room. G-Baby and Handsome were asleep head-to-toe on the bed, and Dreek was sitting in the chair with a PS4 controller in his hand playing Grand Theft Auto 5. "Where Lingo at?" I asked as I sat all the way up with my feet now on the floor.

He yawned showing a big gap between his teeth. "He went to go get us something to eat."

"How long he been gone?"

He put the controller down and stared into space for a second. "Damn, that nigga been gone for a lil' minute."

"How long, Dreek?" I asked more sharply this time.

"I don't know, like a hour and thirty minutes."

I picked up my phone and called him. It just went straight to voicemail. I tried two more times and got the same results. "Fuck!"

"Wassup, big bro'?" G-Baby asked in a groggy voice.

I put my face in my hands. "I think this stupid-ass-nigga Lingo done got himself jammed up."

Handsome popped up. Him and Lingo stayed together 24/7. Where you saw one, you saw the other, so I knew he was all ears now. "By who?"

"That's the million-dollar question right there."

"So, you telling me this nigga just up and disappeared?" Rampage asked in a skeptical tone.

"That's what I said ain't it? We done checked every jail and hospital in and around the city. I'm startin' to think the worst, shawty."

"You think he got kidnapped?"'

"Or whacked."

He looked at me with a knowing look. "Come on, who gone be that stupid? Niggas ain't gone try us like that."

"Niggas just tried to take my whole head off at a gas station. We up there on the food chain, but that don't mean we untryable, my nigga. When you get stripes, it's always somebody looking to earn stripes off you. You should know that better than anybody."

We were in the dining room of his apartment eating lasagna that Shanay and Jasmine cooked for us. They were in the living room feeding the kids while we talked business at the table.

"What we gone do?"

"Nigga, you the Don. You need to be telling me what we gone do."

He sparked a blunt and puffed away. "You supposed to be the Don. I'm just a nigga who whacked some niggas for revenge and ended up earning some stripes."

I motioned for him to pass the blunt. He did it. "I mean... The only thing we really can do is put a lookout on him and wait."

"Shit crazy. Black told me what happened with JD and them. You think it was only them?"

"Positive. If it was anybody else, they would've said something. We took them niggas through the motions before I whacked 'em."

He shook his head sadly. "I'm gone miss that nigga. Lisa gone be devastated."

"You think she gone know you had something to do with it?"

"Nah, I'm gone just play like some other niggas did it. That along with Lingo missing, I'm just gone play it like it might be another war on the way."

I nodded my head and thought about something. "It might be between us and the authorities if you keep pointing guns at police and shit."

"Oh, you heard about that, huh?" He asked with a stupid ass smirk on his face.

"That shit ain't funny, lame-ass-nigga. You put our folks in jeopardy because you wanted to be in yo' feelings. That wasn't no smart shit at all."

"I ain't trying to hear that shit you and Monster talkin'. That fuck-nigga Robo Cop tried me."

I passed him the blunt back and pointed my index-finger at him. "Just like I told that nigga Strong last night, don't let your pride be your downfall. Beat the odds, do numbers, and remain humble. That's the key to success, my brother."

"I feel you on that. I'll try to work on my shit. Speaking of Strong, how that shit go?"

"He said I'm probably the only nigga that could make a nigga feel good about being extorted."

He started laughing and slapping the table. "You flexin', shawty! Ain't no muthafuckin' way that nigga said that out his mouth with all them folks around."

"That's on the 4's. Ask yo' boy Black."

"That shit crazy. You want to go in on a new house?"

He caught me by surprise with that one. "Sound good but give it a few months. Ain't no rush. Don't want niggas to think we going Hollywood on 'em already." I joked seriously.

"Hollywood? We probably two of the realest niggas in the game."

I dapped him up on that one. "Fuck you mean!"

Malik D. Rice

CHAPTER 11
~ Rampage ~

"What's wrong, babe? Why you still sitting at this table? Toe-Tag left two hours ago. What's on your mind?" Jasmine said. She never really knew how to read body language. A blind person could see that I wasn't trying to be bothered right now.

"I got a lot goin' on right now. Shit crazy, shawty."

She sat on the table next to me. "You want to talk 'bout it?"

"No, I don't. You heard from yo' mamma?"

"Never stopped hearing from her. She been blowing me up since the day I left."

"Saying what?"

"You know what she saying. She want me to come back home. How you gone fuck my life up. Oh yeah, can't forget this one. I'm gone end up like Adalis."

I smiled. "Sound 'bout right, she never was my biggest fan. Think I should give her some money to shut her up?"

She thought about it for a moment. "How much you talking?"

"I don't know. What you think she'll sell you to me for?"

"A million dollars." She answered quickly with a wide grin.

"Bitch, I ain't even got a million dollars to myself yet. Even if I did, you got me fucked up. I'm gone bring her $15,000 personally."

She sucked her teeth. "And say what? 'Here. This $15,000. I'm trynna buy yo' daughter. Where's the receipt?' I can hear you now."

"You hell, shawty." I said in between laughter. She was silly as fuck.

"Can you take me out somewhere? I'm tired of sitting around this damn apartment."

"Yeah, just give it a minute. Too much going on right now."

"Whatever you say, baby."

She was playing songs off her phone and the same song AK was just performing at the club last night had came on. "How the hell you get that song on your phone?"

"I downloaded it off SoundCloud. Everybody kept reposting it, so I listened to it. It's nice ain't it?"

I nodded my head to the music. "Shit is hard, can't even lie. I ain't know the nigga had it in him. I'm glad he found something to do because running these streets with me gone be hell for his ass."

She hit me on the shoulder. "Why you be doing that man like that? He was so mad when you made him take us to the mall. I knew he wanted to say no, but yo' mean ass ain't give him no choice."

"He did have a choice. The dumb way and the smart way. He chose the smart way."

"What Toe-Tag said about moving out the hood?"

"He trying to wait until we get our money up some more."

"I can't wait."

"Me neither."

The Dons in Vonte's camp held a meeting amongst themselves every other month to catch up with each other to discuss issues, problems, and solutions. This was my first meeting and I was kind of nervous about it. I never was good with all the politics and what-not, that was more of Toe-Tag's thing. I just did what it did, I never liked talking about it.

The meeting was taking place at one of DG's many chill-spots throughout the city. This one was in a house on Covington Highway that looked ordinary on the outside but was modeled like a club on the inside. Elegant granite floors, high ceilings with diamond chandeliers, and neon lights.

I dressed-to-impress in a tailored mink coat over a nice combination of designer apparels and put on all my jewelry. I wanted them to see how good a young nigga was eating in these streets. I brought my whole kill team with me, and some. They were in the lounge area entertaining the strippers while we were downstairs in the conference room. We sat at a black marble round table in comfortable soft leather seats. You had no choice but to feel like a boss when you sat at this table.

"Alright. Now that everybody's here, we can get started. We got two new faces at the roundtable this month. Don Rampage and Don Spider. Welcome to the round-table." Pablo announced. He was the new Top Don now that Kapo wasn't in the picture anymore. He was an all-around average looking man. Average height, average features, and an average personality to match. The most distinct thing about him was his shoulder-length dreads that he kept dyed bright blonde. He ran a camp that mostly consisted of scammers.

"Good to be here, man. The made man life is the life to live." Said Spider. He was a long stretch of a man standing at about 6'4". He had a nappy 'fro with a tapered fade, and golden skin like an Egyptian. He was Kapo's right-hand-man for the longest. He stayed loyal and consistent. Now he was the Don over a camp that mostly consisted of drug dealers of every kind. The most profitable camp inside of Vonte's.

"You got to know how to balance this made man lifestyle out, or you'll lose control, and everything will fall." Pablo retorted matter-of-factly.

"You ain't never lied." I chimed in, speaking for the first time since I'd been there.

They all looked at me, but it was Pablo that spoke. "If it ain't lil' Rampage. I been waiting to catch up with you for a minute now. You done broke quite a few records in this DG shit. You the biggest legend sitting in this room right now."

"Speak for yourself. That lil' nigga doing his little thing, but

I'm Don Purp Hefner. Everybody know wassup with me." Purp was the type of nigga that could finesse the President's wife to sell pussy for him on a bad day. He was about 5'8" with dark, rich chocolate skin, and long purple dreads that he took great care of. He had the flamboyance of Prince, and the game of Iceberg Slim. He was the only male in his camp. The rest consisted of Dinero Girls that sold themselves for him.

I put both hands in the air in surrender. "Those were his words, not mine. You most definitely a legend in my eyes, big bro. I was hearing stories about you before Dilluminati."

"I appreciate that, youngin'. How you feeling though? Need me to take any of those Dinero Girls off of your hands?" He asked while rubbing his hands together in prayer-position.

I gave him a knowing look. "I'm gone keep my hoes *far* away from you, my guy."

Everybody started laughing.

"Alright, look. Down to business. Vonte got the biggest camp in Atlanta, and he depend on us to keep it running smoothly. He do it by dividing it up into four. A camp for each of us to run. We help each other in any way possible because we're one as a whole. For example, I'll sell Spider some counterfeit to buy some drugs. Or Purp will lend Rampage a few temptresses to lure in one of his targets."

When he said that, a light flicked on in my head. "That sound about right there. Just might work."

"If I put one of my bitches on a nigga, she'll put the pussy on him so good he might kill himself if she consider it."

"Oh, we'll see about that." I said with an evil smirk.

We were on Covington Highway coming from the meeting about to hop on the interstate when I saw a pair of blue lights flashing behind. It was one cruiser trying to pull over two trucks. I called Quay who was in the truck behind us.

He didn't give me a chance to speak before he went to talking. "Just chill. I'm about to take them on a chase when we reach this next light, so y'all can get on the expressway and get ghost."

I wanted to come up with a better solution, but truth was, there wasn't one. He was just doing his job by protecting me. "Y'all niggas do *whatever* y'all got to do to get away. Just make sure y'all don't get caught with those guns in that truck!" I commanded sharply before hanging up with a heavy heart. They were basically about to sacrifice their lives to ensure my safety.

"Toe-Tag in that truck." Said Monster.

"My lil' brother in that truck." Said Black.

"And three more Mobsters with people that care about them too. They going by procedure, y'all know how this shit go. They gone make it, though. We been getting away from the police all our lives."

I saw Black shaking his head through the rearview mirror. "Not out here."

"Y'all niggas just chill. They gone make it!" I assured even though I wasn't too sure. I put my hand on my neck and searched for my chain with the Jesus head on it. When I found it, I pinched the medallion and said a quick silent prayer for my brothers.

Malik D. Rice

CHAPTER 12
~ Quay ~

As soon as we neared the light, it had turned red. I was hoping that it stayed green so I could just breeze on past, but it turned red, so I just said fuck it and burst a U-turn, then gunned it down the opposite street, going back the way we came. Just like I predicted, they were right on our tails. I didn't even have to second-guess about the others getting away. They were gone like vapor.

"Fuckkkk!" Toe-Tag barked so loud that he almost made me lose control of the steering wheel.

"Come on with that shit, man! You just scared the fuck out of me!"

"Ain't no way, shawty!" He spat angrily while hitting the back of my seat.

The police cruiser was on our ass. "Drive this muthafucka, Quay! I ain't going back to jail! That's on the 4's!" G-Baby shouted enthusiastically. He was pumping himself up to do whatever it took to get out of this situation.

I ignored them and turned the music up. One of DG Rell's songs was playing, and it was the perfect tune to be listening to at the moment. Gangster lyrics with a high tempo. I was swerving in and out traffic trying my best to gain a good lead on them.

"Them folks on our ass! We ain't gone be able to lose 'em in this truck!" Handsome shouted over the music.

The fucked-up part about Handsome's statement was that it was one-hundred percent true. I'd been in over ten high-speed-chases, and I was the driver in four of them. So, I wasn't new to this, but this was my first chase in a truck. You couldn't make the same moves in a truck that you could in a small car. I had to come up with a plan real fast. There was a big subdivision full of duplex houses coming up on the right. I started pressing the brakes to slow the truck down and turned the music all the way down.

"What the fuck you doing, nigga? Why you slowing down!" Toe-Tag asked in panic. The cruiser was literally on our bumper.

I looked in the rearview mirror. "It's only one officer in that car. That mean he can't get out." I reached on my lap and passed my Glock over to Handsome, who was in the passenger's seat next to me. "When this car stop, y'all niggas get out with everything and get somewhere."

"What you gone do?" G-Baby asked in a concerned tone.

"What you think, nigga?" I slowed to a stop in front of a patch of woods that led to the subdivision. "Go! Go! Go! Hurry the fuck up!" When they were out of the truck, I pressed the gas pedal so hard that I burned out before taking off down the street, swerving through traffic once again. It was 11:00pm on a Friday, so it was a busy night.

"You got this, Quay." I turned up the music and put my game face on.

At this point, I was just trying to get far away from the subdivision I dropped my brothers off at. They left with all the guns and weed, so I wouldn't get charged with anything but fleeing and alluding. I just hoped my niggas made it somewhere safely because it wasn't a doubt in my mind that they would shoot-it-out if the police caught up with them.

After I cleared a few miles, I wasn't even really speeding anymore. I was just driving, thinking about everything that my life currently consisted of. Money, murder, pussy, drugs, guns, and jewelry. Everything that I always dreamed of as a young nigga. I had more of it than I ever did, but the messed-up part about it is that I barely got to enjoy it because my life or freedom was always in jeopardy. What good was all that shit if I wasn't going to live to enjoy it?

I had three cop cars now following behind me with their lights and sirens on. I was driving so far down Covington Highway that I was nearing Lithonia. I dug in my coat pocket and pulled out the last two grams of Molly I had, popped it into my mouth, and chewed it while it was still in the plastic.

I pulled over, turned the car off, rolled the window down, and put both hands out of it with my palms open. I knew how the police liked to play it, and I most definitely wasn't trying to get shot.

When they closed in with their flashlights and guns on me, I still had a mean mug on my face from the Molly that I took. It was nasty and potent. It had that effect. If I was going to spend a night in jail, I was gone do it high as a kite.

For some reason, while I was on my way to the precinct, all I could think about was my niggas. Not Rampage and the bros in the car with him. I knew they were straight. But it was the bros that were in the car with me I was worried about. Now that I was thinking about it, I should've called one of their phones to see if they would answer, but it was too late for that. All I could do for them now was hope the best for them.

Malik D. Rice

CHAPTER 13
~ Toe-Tag ~

When we hopped out of the truck, we all gunned it into the woods and came out in the backyard of a house in the subdivision. Handsome thought it was a good idea to find shelter in that house, but I told him it wasn't, and we kept pushing. Dreek thought it was a good idea to find shelter in another house in the subdivision, but I told him it wasn't, and we kept on pushing.

I knew from common sense that the officers would be calling back-up to search the area, and the last thing I wanted to do was get caught up in that search. I used to have an aunt that lived in the area, so I knew the area good enough to know that there was another subdivision next to this one, but the houses were whole, they weren't split in half. Which was better for us.

They followed me to the other end of the subdivision, through another patch of woods, where we took a quick breather, across a dark and lonely backstreet, into the other subdivision. The one that I memorized.

I spotted a house on a corner with a purple Audi in the driveway and came up with a quick plan. We were standing across the street from the house on a dark corner in between two houses, so we couldn't be detected easily since all of us were wearing black from head-to-toe.

"Handsome, give me your bag." I demanded urgently. I was tired, out of breath, and ready to sit down somewhere with a big blunt in my mouth.

He looked at me with suspicion. "For what?"

"You need to go to that door and ring the doorbell so we can bomb-rush that muthafucka and have somewhere to stay for the night."

"Why I got to do it?"

87

I looked at him and was surprised he even asked that question. He stayed in the mirror more than my bitch, so I knew for a fact his Chris Brown looking ass knew why he had to be the decoy at a house with a purple car in the driveway. "Come on, man, you the prettiest nigga out here. You the only one they might not be scared to open the door for."

G-Baby nodded his head in agreement. "True."

"Ain't nobody ask your lil' black ass." He spat before taking his bookbag off, shoving it in my arms, and stomping toward the house like a teenage boy whose parents just told him he couldn't go to a Friday night party.

"What if they don't let him in?" G-Baby asked.

"They don't got to. All they got to do is open the door, and the rest is history."

We were ducked on the bottom of the porch while Handsome stood at the door. He rang the doorbell twice, and we all got prepared. We took our AK-47 semi-assault rifles out of our bookbags and waited.

After a long two minutes, somebody came to the door. To my relief, it was a woman. "Who is it!" She yelled through the door, probably looking through the peephole.

"Hey, how you doing, ma'am? I'm so sorry to bother you at this late hour, but I'm really in a bind. My car broke down right in front of the subdivision. Would you mind if I used your phone to make two quick calls? One to get my car picked up, and one to get me picked up." He said in the most proper voice I'd ever heard him talk with.

I was smiling hard on the inside. I could see this stupid ass nigga standing at the door flashing his award-winning smile, trying his best to seduce the lady. The locks started turning, and just like I predicted, the door opened for him.

"Of course, you can use my phone, handsome. And don't worry

about calling anybody to pick you up, I'll—"

We didn't give her a chance to finish the rest of the sentence. When she saw us come running up the stairs with the guns pointed at her, she froze in place. "Get the fuck back, bitch." I spat aggressively, but not too loud. I didn't want to alarm anyone else that might've been in the house. "You scream, you die." I guess G-Baby took that as a signal to wrap an arm around her neck and put a hand around her mouth. I looked her in those pretty blue eyes of hers and motioned for G-Baby to move his hand. "You a pretty lil' white bitch, even for your age. Now, I'm only going to ask you this question once. The truth will set you free, a lie will kill you."

"Anything you want. Just don't kill me." She whispered urgently with tears gliding down her pale face.

"Who else is in the house?"

"Nobody. I live alone. My husband is an architect across seas, so he's never home, and my daughter moved out years ago. I'm all alone."

Dreek came back in the house with the bags and locked the door behind himself. "These houses look better on the inside than the outside." He wasn't lying either, but I doubted every house looked like this on the inside. I believe she just had the inside renovated.

I made G-Baby let her go, and we escorted her to the living room. "Sit down. If you try something stupid, you gone regret it."

She popped-a-squat on one of the smaller couches in the room.

I told Handsome and Dreek to check every inch of the house. When they were gone, I looked at G-Baby whose eyes were already on me looking like a little bad ass cockroach. It looked like he'd just saw a ghost. "What?"

"Look at this bitch." He said while motioning at the lady.

I looked down at her and couldn't believe my eyes. Either they were playing tricks on me, or this lady was really sitting there playing with herself. She had on a cream silk robe that wasn't closed anymore, and she sat there with her legs spread eagle, rubbing her clit with lightning speed, looking up at me and G-Baby savagely. "What the hell you got going on girl?"

She moaned softly. "I can't help it. It's just that you guys are soooo... Gangster. And it turns me way on. I've been fantasizing about getting gangbanged by a group of real thugs for years, and here you guys are, like it's meant to be."

I looked back at G-Baby, but he wasn't looking at me this time. He was locked in on that pretty pink pussy. Neither one of us said a word. We just stood there and watching her rub her clit with one hand, and finger-fucking herself with the other. She had a tight body for a woman her age, everything still looked good, but I knew she had to be at least sixty. I couldn't stick my dick in that lady.

"What the fuck!" Handsome shouted excitedly as he walked back in the living room with Dreek by his side.

"Old freaky ass bitch." Dreek spat jokingly.

"Ohhhhhhh, yes! Talk dirty to me! Somebody choke me. Slap me. Do me dirty!" She came all the way out of her robe and spread her legs farther apart. "I'm all yours's boys! I want dick in every hole on my body."

They were looking back and forth from her to me, waiting to see what move I was going to make. "Y'all niggas go ahead. I'm straight on shawty."

They were still hesitant until G-Baby popped it off. "Shitttt, you ain't got to tell me twice. That's more for me." He walked up to her, grabbed her hair, and dragged her down to the floor on her knees before pulling his wood out, and shoving it into her mouth.

The next thing I knew, two more dicks were in her face. I shook my head with a smile on my face, looking like a proud father, even though Handsome and Dreek was older than me. I sat down on the Laz-E-Boy chair, grabbed the remote, ordered a movie on demand, and tuned them out. Halfway through my movie, I cut my phone on that was on the charger, and I saw about a hundred missed calls from Rampage, Monster, and Black. I was just about to call one of them back when an incoming call popped up from Monster. "Wassup, fat boy?" I answered with a mouth full of buttered popcorn I made in the microwave.

"Yoooo! What the fuck, man? Y'all niggas good? Where y'all at? What happened?" He asked urgently. I could tell my nigga was worried about me.

"Just chill, big bro'. Everything good." I took the phone from my ear and called him on FaceTime. "Look at this shit." I flipped the camera around and pointed it at the porn scene that was taking place on the other end of the living room.

"What the fuck? I hope y'all ain't raping that lady."

I flipped the camera back around to the front so he could see the mug I had on full display. "Stop trying me, nigga! You know I ain't gone let no shit like that happen on my watch. You taught me way better than that."

"So, she asked for it?" He asked in confusion.

"The bitch *begged* for it! G-Baby and Dreek tried to tap out on her, but I made them get back in there. Got to finish what they started."

He burst out into laughter and told Rampage what was going on. "Rampage asked why you ain't get your dick wet."

"Tell that gay ass nigga not to be worrying about my dick." I responded playfully.

"Y'all need somebody to come get y'all?"

I shook my head. "Nah, we good. We gone make it back just fine." I assured while looking at the lady taking one in the ass, and one in the mouth. Something told me she would end up being an asset to the camp. Maybe she was right. It probably was meant for us to pop-up at her house. I definitely believed that everything happened for a reason.

Malik D. Rice

CHAPTER 14
~ Kapo ~

One thing I figured out about life somewhere along the line is that it's not about the situations that you're placed in, it's about what you make of them. I was laying in bed last night after making love to my wife and had to remind myself of the fact. Up until then, I felt burdened and cursed about my current situation, but I had to reevaluate the whole ordeal.

There was really no wrong or right. No good or bad. Everything revolved around perception. I felt bad about the situation because I was perceiving it from a negative point-of-view, but if I were to chance my perception and look at things in a more positive light, I could begin to make the best of it. That's exactly what I did.

I woke up the next morning with plenty of energy and motivation to come up with the perfect plan to turn the tables of the game in my favor. "Please tell me why the maid is sitting on our couch with her feet up watching TV while you're in the kitchen cooking breakfast." I said to my wonderful wife as I walked into our wonderful kitchen, enjoying the aroma of the wonderful food in the air. Every time I looked at her, I always wondered how a beautiful goddess like herself could even fall in love with an ugly hoodlum like myself.

She looked at me and smile brightly, showcasing her bright smile, and it had nothing to do with the braces either. "Because I told her to take a little break. She's always working so hard."

"That is what we pay her for."

She tried to slap me with the greasy spatula in her hand, but I jumped back just in time. "I don't care what she gets paid for, she needs a break, Kareem."

"Whatever you say. You're the boss."

We ate breakfast, enjoying each other's company. You know

you have a soulmate when you never get tired of each other, and the love never fades, just gets stronger. That's a real match. Me and Tanya had been together for over a decade. We weren't even two people anymore; we were basically one. Which is why she was staring at me. She favored Lisa Ray when she put on a serious face.

"You know it's not polite to stare, baby." I reminded sarcastically.

"Keeping things away from your wife isn't either. Now, what is it? Think you got feelings for another stripper?" She asked suspiciously.

I sucked my teeth. "I'll never hear the end of that one. No, baby. This has nothing to do with another female. I'm more than happy with what I have and will never put that in jeopardy again. We already been over this a thousand times before."

"So, what is it then? I know when something isn't right with you, so don't sit here and tell me that it's nothing." She commanded with her arms folded over those juicy watermelons I loved so much.

"It's just work, baby, that's all."

"You still retiring soon, aren't you?"

I remained silent with my eyes on my empty plate.

"Kareem Cooper, I know you hear me talking to you." She barked sounding like a younger version of my mother, who she got along greatly with.

I discussed work with her as long as it had nothing to do with anything incriminating. "This lame ass nigga Freddy gone let Masio promote me to the Pope over Georgia. Now I can't retire because it's too many people depending on me."

She took a hard, deep breath. "Okay. What's the pros and the cons of the situation, other than you not being able to retire."

"I mean, other than me not being able to retire, it puts me at a way higher risk of going to prison. The list of pros are very long. With that much money and power, and a few strategic alliances here and there, I won't have to worry about going to prison. Plus, Masio is a lazy-ass-nigga who wants me to run the camp for him."

"Okay, so that's a good thing. You'll basically be calling all the shots. All you have to do is win their loyalty and you'll be unstoppable. Fear brings hatred, and if someone hates you, there's no limit to what they'll do to bring you down. We can't have that." She stood up, walked over to me, and kissed me softly on the lips. "I always figured that soon would never come, and you'd never retire anyway, so I'm not too rattled about the situation. I want you to know that I'll stand by your side no matter what, but I need you to do your part. I need you to do whatever it takes to stay your yellow ass out of prison. You be the best Pope that they've ever seen and make them love you so much that they'll take a life-sentence for you and protect you with their lives. Even if they never get a chance to meet you." As she walked away, she slid her hand off of my shoulder, down my arm. I loved that lady so much. She knew how to make a nigga feel like a king that could take over the world. She was my fuel, and I was prepared to win the race.

There was a newly built club in Macon, Georgia called Gifted on the westside. It was owned by Fat Head, the Capo for DG over the city. He'd just officially opened the doors a month ago. It was the most talked about spot in the city, and hands-down the most elegant establishment they had in town.

I walked inside the place with the new shadows that I purchased from D.W. Security Company. Most of the big made men in Dilluminati shopped for their security there. I only ordered two guards and nicknamed them Glock and Bullet. Both had impressive military backgrounds, and a reputation for being fiercely loyal. Exactly what I needed.

Glock was a short, close-built black man with muscles in every part of his body. Bullet was an athletically built white man that stood two feet taller than me at 6'2". I hope they turned out to be worth the money I was paying for them.

As we stood in front of the club's security waiting for a waitress to lead us to my VIP section, I leaned close to Glock's ear. "You think y'all could take them?"

He scanned the club's security unimpressively. "I could take them by myself. Would you like a demonstration?" He asked with a straight face. There was no trace of humor in his voice. He was dead serious.

I shook my head with a sly grin. "Nah, you good. The time will come for that. Just make sure you show out then."

"You got it, boss."

I pulled the collar up on my pea coat. It felt like Alaska outside. As soon as I was about to ask where the waitress was, a dark-skinned beauty showed up in a sparkling black Hooter's-like outfit. "Please follow me this way." She said while trembling under the cold wind and rushed back inside with us on her tail. She us led through the thick crowd, a door, and down a hall that was lined with doors on both ends. We followed her all the way to the end of the hall where a door sat. "Welcome to the Presidential VIP section. The main event rapper and his entourage usually uses this section, but not today. Who are you, if you don't mind me asking?" I could tell by the sparkle in her eyes that she was eager to know.

The sparkle in her eyes wasn't because of my looks. I looked like a light skinned version of Jay-Z. It was because of my prestige. Most women, especially her age, would fall in love with any man they thought could get them to where they needed to be. I flashed a smile at her. "I'm God's son." I answered before opening the door and walking into the most exquisite VIP room I've ever stepped foot in. "They went all-out with this place." I looked around at the spacious room with spotted black granite floors, sexy furniture, a full bar, and a stage with two stripper poles on it.

Glock and Bullet insisted on standing guard outside of the door so they could keep track of the movement in the hallway. Of course, I let them go ahead. I was fixing myself a drink at the bar when Bullet stuck his head through the door. "Party of three requesting to enter. One Fat Head, and two unknown."

"Let them in."

"You got you a mean security detail right there." A big, bald man with a boulder sitting on top of his shoulders stated. That had to be Fat Head.

"I can get used to them. They're expensive, but they mean business." I held up my drink. "Want a drink?"

They all sat down. "Just bring a bottle of Hennessey with you." Fat Head said with a wave of his hand.

I grabbed a serving tray and put the bottle on it with my drink and a few extra cups. I sat the tray down on a black granite table that seemed to come out of the floor, grabbed my drink, and took a seat on the sleek wraparound sofa.

"That's a nice suit right there. Where can I get one of those?" An older cat asked with interest. He had sideways waves with a salt and pepper beard, and brown skin that was in the first stages of becoming wrinkled.

I looked down at my black, foreign designer threads. "I got this one custom made at Armani. It's one of my favorite ensembles. You must be Sampson?"

"The one and only. Nice to meet you, youngin." He was the Capo over the city of Albany.

"The pleasure is all mine. It's nice to meet all three of y'all."

Fat Head nodded his boulder. "We're happy to have you. We never really used to meet with Masio, and when we did meet with Drop Top, we all had to travel to Atlanta. I'm glad to have you at my club."

"I'm happy to be here. This is a beautiful establishment right here. Take care of it. But that's the type of shit I want to discuss right there. Things are about to start changing from this day forward."

"What kind of changes? And why isn't Masio or Freddy here?"

"Masio's not here because he has me running Georgia for him, so he won't have to do shit. He's the opposite of Drop Top. Freddy's not here because this meeting doesn't concern him. He's only concerned with the welfare of his city. I'm here with y'all because I do care. I believe y'all been unappreciated for too long, and I'm here to open the door for y'all. I just need one thing in return."

"And what's that? More money than what y'all already extorting us for?" A Hispanic man with a nasty scar running down the side of his face asked accusingly. He had to be QP. The Capo over the city of Augusta.

I chuckled softly. "No."

"Then, what do you want, young man? Spit it out." Sampson commanded.

"Loyalty."

Fat Head took a swig straight from the bottle. "So, you trying to form an alliance with us or something?"

"No. I'm trying to form a family."

CHAPTER 15
~ Rampage ~

I had Lisa blowing my phone up trying to see if I found the people responsible for JD's death. It turned out Lingo got snatched up by the feds, who held him in an interrogation room for 48 hours without any communication. The gun he had on him was dirty, and they hung a murder over his head, trying to get him to spill the beans on the rest of the camp. He stayed solid. I had his mother and big sister blowing my phone up trying to see if I was going to get him a lawyer that could get him out. Quay's big sister, Monique, was knocking on my door. I told Jasmine to let her in.

She came in with Quay on her heels.

"I tried to tell her I was gone pay her back." He said before she could get a word out.

"I need $1,500, Rampage. I just bonded this lil' nigga out for some shit he did for you." Monique spat while standing in front of me and blocking my view of the television.

"Man, you know it ain't no pressure on no money, but gotdamn, Quay. You couldn't clear $1,500? You in violation nigga. You a Mafioso. You supposed to keep at least $25,000 tucked somewhere."

He averted eye contact because he knew he was in the wrong. Ain't no way his sister was supposed to be standing in my living room, interrupting the little peace time that I did get to enjoy.

"In between my kids, my family, clothes, and jewelry, it didn't leave me with much. And the little $8,000 that I did have on me, they took, bro."

I reached in my Gucci bag and pulled out $2,000 for Monique. "Here. You like family, so I ain't gon' trip about you pushing up in here like you did, but don't ever do that again. All you had to do was send word, and you know I would've straightened that little shit."

She nodded her head. "My bad, lil' bro. These damn kids and they daddy just got me so frustrated, and then this lil' nigga call me telling me to bond him out. I'm just stressed out, man."

"I know the feeling. If you ever need something, just let me know."

"Thank you."

"This my hood. That's what I'm here for."

She walked out, and Quay tried to follow her, but I stopped him in his tracks. "Come here, Quay. I got to talk to you."

Monique chuckled and waved at him before leaving. He stopped in his tracks and walked back over toward me.

"Sit down, nigga."

He sat down on the couch next to me. "I'm gone pay you back, bro. Every penny."

"No shit. I already know that. That's not what I called you back for."

He slanted his already slanted eyes even more. "What's up then? Talk to me."

"I need you to go send a message for me. Go take this money to Lingo's people for his lawyer. Then, I need you to pull up on Handsome. Tell that nigga that he gon' be responsible if Lingo ever decides to get the loose lips because he introduced that nigga to the camp."

"Alright, bro'. Anything else?"

"Tell Toe-Tag to bring the truck around. I got another meeting with Vonte. I'm bringing him this time."

Me and Toe-Tag walked into a Presidential Suite inside of the W Hotel on Peachtree Avenue. The sexy model that had answered the door was just the tip of the iceberg. There were beautiful vixens all throughout the place. Some were entertaining one of Vonte's men, while others just sitting around on their phones looking gorgeous.

Vonte was on the floor in the main living room playing 2K15, while a brown skinned barbie doll with tattoos everywhere sat on the sofa behind him. She was braiding his dreads together, making them thicker.

His top shooter, Silent, looked at us unimpressively.

"Wassup?" I greeted, but he didn't pay me any attention. He just focused back on the game.

I wanted to say something about the disrespect, but I knew enough about Silent not to try him. The rumor was that he came from a Haitian family that manipulated black magic or some shit. Either way, I didn't want any problems with the nigga.

"His name is Silent for a reason. Y'all niggas take a seat. I don't like talking to niggas while they standing over me."

We sat down on the sofa. "Wassup, big bro'? What you need?"

He paused the game and tapped the girl's leg. She got up and walked off with ass jiggling everywhere in the fishnet shorts that were hugging her ass.

"Just trying to see how you living, lil' nigga. You handling that business out there too."

I looked over at my boy, Toe-Tag and thought this was as good of a time as any to put him in the game. "I ain't gone lie. If it wasn't for my nigga right here, a lot of shit would've never gotten done. He the brains, and the muscle."

Vonte looked at him sideways. "Brains and muscle. You usually don't find niggas with both characteristics too often. What's your name?"

"Toe-Tag."

That earned a chuckle, and a smile out of Silent.

"Ain't no way?" He looked over at Silent in surprise and back at Toe-Tag. "I think he likes you."

Toe-Tag smiled devilishly. "Whatever that's supposed to mean."

"I fuck with y'all lil' bad ass niggas. We ain't too far apart in age. I'm only 18. The only reason I'm sitting in my spot is because of my brother and my uncle."

We nodded in understanding.

"Anyway." He took a sip from a doubled Styrofoam cup that was most likely filled with Lean. "Y'all niggas been handling that business in the field. I got another mission for y'all."

"From now on, we charging a ticket on everybody. Ten or better." I informed uneasily. I wasn't sure how he would react, but it was something I had to do.

He laughed with both hands in the air in surrender. "Aight, gangsta. You got it. But that's not what this is. It's this psychotic ass nigga named, No Brain, from Griffin, Georgia. He run a set of Bloods called Zoo Krew in Spaulding Heights. They spreading they wings, and it's starting to interfere in some of our territories. I need y'all to have a talk with that nigga."

I looked at Toe-Tag and he just shrugged his shoulders, meaning he didn't care. "If that nigga high profile like you say, why you sending us?"

"I got my reasons. If you can't persuade him to do it, then he gone have to answer to me."

"Them niggas got a mean movement. You really think they gone fall up under this DG shit?" Toe-Tag asked curiously.

Vonte shook his head. "No. I don't want him to fall up under us. I just want him to join forces. You know the saying."

Me, and Toe-Tag nodded. "If you ain't with us, you against us." We said in unison.

"We got to watch out for that nigga, Vonte." Toe-Tag

suggested.

We were in the Escalade on the way back from the meeting. He was behind the wheel, while I fucked around on one of my phones in the back. "What make you say that?" I asked seriously. If Toe-Tag had a bad feeling about somebody, it was usually right.

"He a slime ball. I don't trust that nigga. He don't give a fuck about us. All he care about is Ronte and power. That nigga don't even give a fuck about his mamma."

"Shit, I don't give a fuck about my mamma."

"That's different. Your mamma did some foul shit, and she know it."

Blurry flashbacks started to resurface. I shook my head rapidly and pushed them back down into the pit that they belonged in. "What's the point, man?"

"The point is, he's gone use us as much as we let him. We can't become slave to no nigga like that. Our lives gone be a living hell."

"Umm... If you ain't notice, our life's ain't never been too far from it anyway. At least now, we got all this money, drugs, and other shit to dull the pain. Plus, we already slave to that nigga. We in his camp. What you want me to do?"

I could see him shaking his head through the rearview mirror. "I don't know, man. It's got to be a way."

"Yeah, death. Let me know when you find another route. I don't know about you, but I got too much life to live."

Now that I was starting to think about it, I really didn't want to leave the projects. This is the only place I really felt safe at. I could care less about a big house on a hill. I'll have a million dollar car parked right outside my $450 apartment. Some may call it ignorant, but it made perfect sense to me. Jasmine's gone be mad when I break the news to her, but she'll get over it.

Toe-Tag dropped me off in front of my mother's building, and sped off. I had no idea where he was going, and I didn't ask. He did what he wanted to do and he earned the privilege.

I knocked on my mother's door like the police. "Hold the fuck up! Who the... Oh, hey brother." Babie said gently. She literally just went from 100 to 0.

I walked past her and into the apartment. "You was ready to chew somebody head off, wasn't you?"

"I thought you was my ex. I just broke up with his sorry ass a few days ago. Now, he acting like it's the end of the world." She informed, while putting the locks back on.

I gave her a knowing look. "You too young for all that shit."

"Boy, we got the same daddy. You know wassup." She said while twerking her little booty to the music playing from the portable speaker on the table. She had her tongue sticking all the way out.

"Bitch, I'll kill you!" I barked trying to grab her but she ran to the back into the room she shared with Kamya. Kamya was on her bed watching a movie on the new iPad that I just bought for her.

Babie was screaming like a mad woman. "Kamya! Kamya! Raylo trying to hurt me!" She jumped on Kamaya's bed behind her.

Kamya jumped up, and wrapped her arms around me tightly. "Heyyyyyy, beautiful brotherrrr! You trying to kill the little Babie again?"

"That ain't no damn baby. She a grown ass slut."

Babie threw a pillow that hit both of us. "Sorry, Kamya, but fuck you Raylo!" She spat with a middle finger in the air.

Kamya pushed me out of the room while I mouthed threats at Babie. "Where yo' ugly ass mamma at?"

"Stop being so mean. Do you have anything nice to say about anyone?"

"You probably the only one in this house. Where she at, though?"

She shrugged her shoulders. "I don't know. She was gone when we woke up."

"I don't know why she had kids if she ain't trying to take care of them."

"She said we grown. We supposed to take care of ourselves."

I pursed my lips together. "Come on, man. We been taking care of ourselves longer than I can remember. I been the man of this house since I came out the womb."

"The rent lady came today and asked for mamma." She was flipping through the channels on TV trying to find something to watch. She loved movies and TV shows with a passion.

I sat down on the couch next to her.

"You staying for a while?" She asked while looking at me through hopeful eyes.

"Yup. I got to talk to yo' mamma."

She smiled and laid down with her head resting in my lap while I played in her dreads.

"Raylo! Mamma outside in that grey car with that man I was telling you about." Babie informed, while looking out the window in the living room.

Kamya fell asleep on my lap, and I dozed off right after her. I popped up, and rushed over to the window. "Right there?"

"Yup."

I pulled the hood from my sweater over my head and rushed out the door without even grabbing my jacket. I already had my Glock 23, that's all I needed.

I flew down the stairs like a bullet and speed walked to the grey Jaguar that Babie pointed out. I walked right up on the car and opened the passengers door. "Get the fuck out, hoe. Got yo' kids in the house by themselves while you out here trickin' off with this bum ass nigga!"

"Raylo, get the fuck up out my face with that shit. They know how to take care of their self. Stay out of my fuckin' business."

I looked down at the light skinned devil in front of me and just snapped. "Bitch, get out this car!" I grabbed her by the arm and drug her out of the car.

The nigga was a big fat nigga and about my mother's complexion. I never saw him get out of the car, and I damn sure didn't see him sneak up behind me and snatch me up in a bear hug.

"Anybody ever tell you about putting your hands on a lady?"

I saw my mother look past us with wide eyes, but I didn't see Monster crack the nigga's skull with a bat. Fat Joe released his grip and fell down to his knees after Monster caught him in the leg. "Aghhhhhh!"

I landed on my feet. I had plans on taking the bat from Monster and going to work on the nigga, but a gang of Mobsters appeared out of thin air. They started doing him so dirty that I left it alone.

"Leave him alone! Stoppppppp!'' My mother screamed at the top of her lungs.

"Bitch, shut the fuck up! Let's go." I grabbed her by the arm and basically dragged her away from the scene and up the stairs into the apartment.

Babie was at the window cheering the Mobsters on like a loyal football fan, whose team was winning by a landslide. Kamya was on the couch with her face in her hands, crying like she did every other time somebody got hurt around her. She hated violence, and my mother was cursing me out something serious.

I wanted to take my gun out and put a round into the ceiling like they did in the movies, but this wasn't a movie. I would never shoot a gun around my sisters if I didn't have to. I settled for the glass bread bowl on the kitchen counter. I grabbed it, held it high over my head, and slammed it to the ground so hard it made all three of them jump. "Everybody shut the fuck upppp! Gotdamn, I can't even hear myself think."

Babie chuckled. "Shit, that nigga can't either." She said,

referring to the man who was still outside taking an ass whoopin' and yelling at the top of his lungs.

"Babie, please shut the fuck up." I spun on my mother. "What the fuck you do with that money I gave you for the rent?"

"That nigga was just about to give me the rent money before you came and fucked it all up."

I wanted to choke her but I spared her for my sister's sake. "I'm gone ask you one more time. What you do with the money?"

She looked me dead in the eyes with that same look she'd been giving me ever since I caught her snorting a line of cocaine off of some random nigga's dick when I was nine. "I bought a quarter ounce and got higher than Whitney." She answered with a smug smirk on her face.

I nodded my head in understanding. "Kamya, Babie. Y'all go pack y'all shit up."

"Un-uh! Where we going?" Babie asked.

"Y'all comin' with me."

"You ain't takin' my muthafuckin' kids nowhere, nigga."

I walked over to the window and lifted it up. "Dlattttt!" I spat as loud as I could.

The Mobsters instantly stopped their assault, looked up at me in the window, and rushed upstairs to answer the call of distress. I opened the door for them. "You, and you. Go take my sisters to my apartment."

Kamya went and grabbed her coat with no problem, but I had to threaten Babie. She loved my mother's no-good ass. Kamya did too. She just was more scared of me than she was of my mother, so she wouldn't listen to me first. I made Monster wrap my mother in a bear hug to stop her from pulling my sister's back. When they were out of the apartment, and out of the way, I told Monster to let her go.

She flexed her arms, walked up to me, and spit in my face. "I fuckin' hate yo' bitch ass! You think you somebody, nigga? You ain't shit! You gone die in these streets just like yo' daddy, fuck nigga!" She spat from the heart. She never liked me because I reminded her too much of my father.

I wiped my face with the sleeve of my sweater. "The only reason you alive right now is because you my mamma." I moved with snake speed as I connected my hand with her neck and backed her up against the wall. "I'm gone tell you this one time, and one time only. If you ever step foot inside this hood again, you gone die! And you can get high all you want in hell."

"Fuck you!" She managed to say with a tremendous struggle.

"You can't fuck me, sick bitch. I'm your son, but you can leave me." I let her go and she fell to the ground with her hands on her neck, gasping for air.

I turned around and walked out of the apartment like I wasn't fazed by the situation, but deep down inside, I was hurting bad. It pained me to have to do her like that. A lady that I used to love and adore so very much. She made me hate her. She was the first woman to break my heart, and the last woman I would ever love one hundred percent.

I never vented on the problem, but I always longed for a mother that loved me unconditionally like she was supposed to. I longed for a lot of things, but I guess life wasn't Burger King. You couldn't just have shit your way. You just had to work with the cards you were dealt. Sad, but true.

CHAPTER 16
~ Toe-Tag ~

I convinced Rampage to let me and Monster pull up on this nigga, No Brain, by ourselves. Me, and Monster worked better alone. Plus, I didn't want to pull up too deep, painting the wrong picture. Vonte made it clear that he didn't want us to press him into fucking with us. He wanted us to convince him. Another reason why I didn't want Rampage here. He didn't have too much finesse. He was more of a pressure applying type of guy. From the homework I did on No Brain, he wasn't the type of nigga you even thought about pressing.

He even had Monster on edge and big bro didn't get rattled easily. "This is a muthafuckin' suicide mission. I wish I was there. I would've told Vonte to suck my dick." He ranted.

We were pulling up into Spaulding Heights Apartments. Niggas were all over the fucking place. The street nigga in me had to wonder if we were going to make it back out of here alive. We paid a crack smoker from the hood off to borrow her 2001 Ford Taurus for the trip. We didn't want to attract any attention.

I glanced over at him in the passenger's seat. "You would've told him that for real?"

"My screws might not be all the way tightened but they still there. You know I'm just talking shit."

"I know that's right but this nigga No Brain ain't got but a few screws and them muthafuckas dangling out."

"What's the plan? You never told me about that."

I drove over a speed bump and found a random parking spot. "I ain't tell you about a plan because it ain't no plan, nigga. How the hell you make a plan for a conversation with a nigga that's unpredictable?"

He shrugged. "You got a point right there."

"I know. Now, let's get this shit over with."

We hopped out of the car. As soon as both of our doors were closed, we had three pistols trained on us. "Y'all niggas in the wrong hood, ain't it? I hope y'all ain't let no bitch trick y'all out here." A freckle faced man asked, then stated.

We had our hands up. "Nah, big dawg. We here for No Brain on behalf of Dilluminati. We don't mean no harm; we just want to talk to him."

This was the only part I had planned since Vonte didn't know exactly what building No Brain was in. All he told us was that he basically never leaves the apartment complex, so this was the only way we'd get to him.

"Dilluminati? What y'all want to talk to No Brain about? I know how y'all get down. We ain't going for that extortion shit. Y'all must ain't heard about this Zoo Krew shit?" He asked heatedly.

"Of course, we heard about y'all. Y'all making a helluva name in these streets. We not trying to extort y'all. I'm only trying to explain this once, so can you please call yo' boss man so we can get this over with?"

Twelve minutes later, we were escorted about seven buildings down at gunpoint. It was broad daylight but that didn't put me any more at ease. Something told me that nobody would care if they gunned us down in the street right then and there.

We were escorted to an upstairs apartment that was guarded by two men, who were openly carrying fully automatic assault rifles. One of them patted us down and took our pistols. "You'll get these back if you make it out."

The other one opened the door. "Good luck."

We walked into the apartment uneasily. I didn't miss the if in the niggas statement that patted us down, and I'm sure Monster didn't either.

There were men and woman scattered throughout the place minding their own businesses. I was about to ask which one of them was No Brain until a bald muscular brown skinned man walked out from the back. "Dilluminati, huh?"

I looked him up and down. "You're No Brain?"

"If we sent a couple of shooters to y'all hood, would y'all have let them sit down with your Godfather?"

I shook my head.

"Okay then, that should answer your question. I'm OG Hitman. Who am I talking to?"

"I'm Toe-Tag and this is my big brother Monster."

"Some helluva names." He looked around the apartment in disgust. "Y'all muthafuckas see I got company in here trying to talk business! They ain't got nowhere to sit 'cause y'all crowded in this bitch like some sardines! This ain't no homeless shelter! Get the fuck out!" His voice boomed like he was talking through an intercom.

They were taking their time leaving and he snapped again. "Hurry the fuck up before I get mad!" That seemed to put a little pep in their step. I was guessing he wasn't the type of nigga you wanted to see mad.

"Y'all go ahead and take a seat. Want something to drink or snack on?"

I shook my head after taking a seat on the couch. "Nah, I'm good big dawg. I just wanted to chop it up with you for a second, if that's possible."

He took a seat on the arm on the other couch. "Talk."

"We strong believers that if you not with us, you against us. With that being said, y'all been cutting into our territories and we just want to know if we can come up with a solution."

"What you got in mind?"

"Cut off your old supplier and buy from us. Lower prices, better product."

We getting our weed from the bros out in California. We can't cut them off but we getting our Cocaine and Molly from some Haitian connect out of Miami. If y'all can handle him and beat his prices, then we won't have no problem buying from y'all."

"I'll have to talk with my superior and get back at you. You got a number I could reach you at?"

He shook his head. "Just find me the same way you did this time. Should be easier now that you know what building I'm in, and my lil' homies know you not a threat."

We got up to leave.

"Oh, yeah. One more thing."

I turned around. "What's that, OG?"

"Come by yourself next time. I don't like the way big boy looking at me. He might not walk up out of here a second time."

***

I called Quay and told him to pick Shanay up and take her to an address that I sent him. The address belonged to a five-star restaurant downtown called Bizzy's. Everybody was talking about this restaurant, including Shanay. She mentioned it last week, the last time I hit her with the round house special. I had a little extra time on my hands, plus I was missing my woman, so I decided to take her out on a surprise date.

She walked into the place looking ghetto fabulous in her burgundy Monclear coat, blue Robin jeans, and wheat colored Timberlands on. Her long weave was flat ironed how I liked it. She was my type of bitch, hands down.

When she saw me, her eyes lit up and she rushed over to the table I sat at. I looked just as ghetto as she did in the fancy restaurant.

She walked up to me and hit me hard on the shoulder, before taking a seat across from me. "Why the hell you ain't tell me I was coming here? I would've dressed up. We the only people in here looking like this." She said in concern, while looking around at all the bougie ass people, who were sneaking glances at us ever chance they got.

"I ain't tell you because I ain't want you to pull up trying to impress these folks. I wanted to see you how I like you, and I like you just like that, shawty."

"Awwww." She leaned across the table and gave me a wet kiss. "How did you get reservations to this place? They said that you have to call days in advance."

I looked at her like she was crazy. "You know damn well I ain't do all that shit. Yo' nigga a real finesser. I pulled up and used the fuck out of my DG card." I joked seriously.

"What you say, baby?" She asked open mouthed.

I laughed inwardly. My baby was like a big ass kid. She was always in for a good ole story. "Man, I walked right up in this bitch with my game face on and Monster was right behind me. You know his game face always on."

"I'm trying to tell you." She shook her head. "Where is he?"

"Same place as Quay. In the parking lot, sitting in the car. We walked up in this bitch and the lady asked me, do I got a reservation? I made sure I held my head high so she could see the DG on my neck, and I asked her does she know who Freddy is? When I mentioned Freddy's name, her eyes got wide, so I bossed up real fast. I told her to call the manager up there, and he better not keep me waiting."

Her mouth was still open and she was locked in on me, most likely picturing me acting out the story I was telling. "So, what the manager say?"

"He came rushing up to the front with his so called game face on, but I broke that nigga down quick. I grabbed him by the arm and led him to a corner. We was facing a wall. I told that nigga that I was Freddy's security and I was here to meet his daughter for our anniversary. I told him I had forgot all about it until a few hours ago. I told him I needed his help, pulled out my bankroll, and tried to give him a few thousand."

"He took it?"

I shook my head. "He just shook his head and waved his hands. He said he knew how it was to forget an anniversary, and since I was dating Freddy's daughter, the date was on the house."

"Ain't no muthafuckin' way, Tevin. You a real con artist, boy."

I smiled back at her. "I just know how to use what I got to get what I want."

"Mmm-hmm. Just like you used that dick to get my heart?"

"Damn, you got me. My cover's blown." I said with a hand over my face, making her laugh. It drew a few stares, but we didn't care. We were in our own little bubble. I felt sorry for anyone trying to pop it.

CHAPTER 17
~ Jasmine ~

"You couldn't just leave Babie there by herself? She like fifteen goin' on twenty anyway." I told Rampage, while he laid in the bed playing with Karma.

"Just chill. I'm about to make the people next door move into my mamma's old apartment and let them move into the one next door, so I can keep a close eye on them." He informed.

I looked at him awkwardly. "The Spanish lady and her husband? How you just gone make those people move out of their home? How you know they don't like the place they got?"

"They like whatever place is two months' rent free and that's my mamma's old spot."

I shook my head. "Who you think you is throwing all this money around?"

"I think I'm Big Meech! Larry Hoover!" He sang while tickling Karma making her laugh.

I couldn't help but picture him playing with our children. "When you gone get me pregnant, Ray?"

"Most bitches just pull the birth control trick, or stick holes in the condom. You just ask a nigga."

I flashed a mug at him. "I'm not most bitches and you know that. I'm not trying to steal a baby from you. I want you to give me one."

"Let me see how you take care of this one, first."

"So, you using a human being as a lab test?"

"Sound bad when you say it, but yeah." His phone rung, and he answered it.

He said yeah four times, then told them he was on the way.

"Who was that?"

"Don't worry about it. Just know I got to go. I'll be back sooner or later." He kissed me, and Karma before getting up and getting dressed.

Babie went to one of her friend's apartments in the apartment complex down the road, which was fine with me because I didn't want to be around her just as much as she didn't want to be around me. Me and Kamya were in the living room watching a movie when I got a call on my cell phone. It was my mother. "Hey."

"I'm surprised you're still alive."

"How can I help you, ma?" I asked with a roll of my eyes. She'd been working my last nerves lately.

"Just checking on you. I would like to speak to the boy who stole my daughter away from me."

"He's supposed to be pulling up on you soon. He got something for you."

She sucked her teeth. "I don't want that boy's drug money. I just want to look him in his eyes and let him know that if anything ever happens to you, I'll bring him down myself."

"He's not a drug dealer, ma. And ain't nothing gone happen to me, I'm good. I don't know why you keep worrying. You got that money I put in your mailbox?"

"Whatever. That's the devil's money, I know that much. And yeah I got it. It's in your room in your dresser, waiting for you whenever you decide to come visit."

I laughed inwardly. She was so damn stubborn. I guess that's where I got it from. "I'll come visit as soon as I can. I be so busy keeping the house clean and taking care of this baby and this puppy."

"He got you taking care of his child?"

"Raylo don't got no kids. This somebody else baby. It's a long story, but I'm gone have to call you back."

"Alright, girl. Be safe. I love you."

"I love you too, ma." I hung up the phone.

"I can't talk to my mamma because Raylo made her leave us." Kamya informed sadly.

I brought her in for a hug. "You mad at your brother?"

"No, I'm not. I know Raylo loves me more than our mamma does, but it still makes me sad because I'm worried about my mamma. I can't look after her no more."

"She gone be alright. Yo' mamma know how to take care of herself."

"I hope so because if something happen to her, then I'm going to be mad at Raylo."

Shanay came over to my spot with Lil' Tee so he could play with Karma. They got along well and enjoyed each other's company. Just like me and Shanay was beginning to enjoy each other's company.

"Bitch, this nigga finessed his way into a free dinner at Bizzy's. We ordered all the expensive ass shit, took pictures, and had us a good ole time. That shit meant a lot to me."

I would be lying to myself if I said I wasn't a little jealous. "I wish Rampage non-romantic ass would do something special like that for me." I pouted playfully, but I was serious.

"It's alright, he'll come around. You know that young nigga got a lot on his plate."

"Yeah, I know. Aye, can I ask you something?"

"Yeah, wassup girl?"

"Why you think I keep having these dreams about Adalis?"

She shrugged her shoulders. "Like I said, it's probably just your guilty conscience."

I shook my head. "I think that bitch haunting me."

"Really?" She looked at me through slanted eyes.

"Man, that's why I didn't want to say shit. You think this shit funny, but it's something wrong for real."

She threw her hands up. "What you want me to do? I guess

dead bitches get jealous too." She said with a smile.

"Fuck you! I bet you won't be laughing when that hoe kill me in my sleep."

"So, what you gone do? Leave her man alone?"

It was my turn to look at her like she was stupid. "Bitch, please. I'll start popping Molly to stay up more before I do that."

"Good luck with that."

CHAPTER 18
~ AK ~

I was sitting in between one of my girl's legs while she braided my dreads back. I had a show tonight and she was getting me right.

"So, how does it go? Do you have to reach out to DG Records with your music or they have to reach out to you?" She asked interestedly.

"They got to reach out to you. My song trending right now, so it shouldn't be long. They need to hurry up because I'm trying to make it out this shit here."

"What if another record label offers you a deal first?"

"They won't."

"How you so sure?"

"Because I'm Dilluminati. It's already understood that anybody under the DG brand is off limits to any other record label, but DG records."

She whistled. "Damn, I never knew that. Dinero stingy with his people."

"Most definitely. I'm getting offered $5,000 a show right now. That's enough to fall back and focus on rapping, but that ain't gone happen."

"Why?"

"Because in order for me to fall back, I got to ask my Don, which is Rampage."

She took a long breath and pulled my head back so I was looking up at her. "Maybe you should ask him anyway. You never know, he might go for it. You said he don't like you right? He might let you fall back just so you won't be around anymore."

"It ain't gone work, I'm telling you. I rather just keep making songs when I can and doing shows when I can."

"You missed a show yesterday because you was on a mission.

If you don't fall back, you won't enjoy the full extent of the industry world."

An hour later, I was standing in front of Rampage's building contemplating on going through with it, or not. All those old sayings about a man's pride holding him back was true. Especially, a nigga like me coming from where I'm coming from.

It was just my luck that a black Benz truck pulled up in front of the building. Rampage hopped out the back, while Black, got out the driver's seat. I locked eyes with Rampage, and lost all the little hope I did have. Ain't no way I actually thought that this nigga would give me a pass after all I put him through. I could literally see the hatred in his eyes. My mother used to always tell me to watch how I treat people because you'd never know who you need in the future, but obviously I didn't listen.

"Either you got a message for me, or you got something to say to me." Rampage stated arrogantly.

I thought about making up an excuse why I was standing in front of his building and going back to my baby mother's spot, but something made me stick to my guns. "I need to talk to you really quick."

"I ain't got too much time right now. It can't wait until another time?"

"I know you busy, my nigga but it'll be quick. I ain't gone take up too much of your time."

He nodded his head. "Talk to me."

"Right here?" I asked while looking at Black, who was standing right next to us.

"Yeah, right here. right now. Wassup?"

"I know we ain't the best of friends, but I need you right now. I feel like I can't prosper in the rap game if I don't start putting my all in it, and I can't put my all in it unless I fall back. So, I'm standing right here asking you man to man, can you give me a pass to fall back?"

He stood there with an unreadable face, staring me dead in the eyes. I just knew he was going to spazz out on me, but to my surprise, he didn't.

"When you sign yo' deal just don't forget about a nigga."

I blinked my eyes a few times with a blank face. I was trying to see if I heard him right. "So, you gone let me fall back?"

"Yeah, nigga. Just make sure you shout me out on one of them songs." He joked.

"I'm gone do that tomorrow." I promised enthusiastically.

"Oh, yeah. If you don't get signed in four months, I'm gone need you back in the field. You need to be goin' hard in the meantime."

I flashed an evil smirk. "Oh, they gone sign me. I'm gon' go harder than hard."

Malik D. Rice

CHAPTER 19
~ Toe-Tag ~

"What you doing up so late? Come back to bed." This Dominican video vixen said while hugging me from behind.

I stood at the wall length hotel window, looking 60 stories down at the bustling city below. "Get off me, man." I shrugged my shoulders aggressively, making her take a step back.

"What's your problem?"

I turned around and looked at her sideways. "No. What's your problem? You the one out of line, trying to cuddle and shit. We fucked. It is what it is, that's all it's gone be."

"So, you just used me for a nut?"

"Now, you starting to use yo' lil' brain. What you thought? We was gone fall in love and ride off into the sunset? Bitch, please."

Her eyes got misty. "You don't have to disrespect me. If you don't want to be with me that's cool, but you should've let me know this was going to be a one night stand. I would've made you pay."

I laughed inwardly, but on the outside, I was stone cold. "You got exactly forty-four seconds to get yo' shit and get the fuck up out of my hotel room. Before you have to pay the surgeon to fix yo' face."

She stood there and waisted six seconds looking at me, more than likely wondering if I would live up to my words. I guess she wasn't trying to find out, because she rushed to the room, got dressed, and got the fuck out.

When she was gone, I turned back around and looked back down at the city. I caught a glimpse of the view in Vonte's suite when I went to visit him with Rampage, and promised myself that I would get me a similar suite soon. Now, here I was.

I finessed the hotel manager into giving me a room on the house and finessed the model out of some free pussy. I was quickly learning my full potential and abilities. Most of the time, I was just trying shit to see what I could get away with and it was working out for me.

I didn't have a problem paying my dues to Dilluminati because I was using it to get ahead in life. That's what the Godfathers persuaded us to do. A lot of niggas underestimated themselves because they weren't made men but not me. I don't need made man stripes to determine my worth.

If more niggas in DG thought like me, Dinero Guys would be taking over the world in no time.

I left the hotel later on that morning after the sun was in the sky, and it was right back to the business as usual. I had a black 2012 Chevy Impala, rented by one of the older Dinero Girls. I convinced her to do that with her own money.

I sat in the backseat by myself while she drove me around. The back windows were tinted and there was a lesser chance that the police would pull a woman over alone in a car than a young black man with tattoos all over. I came to the conclusion that I had to start moving smarter if I wanted to stay in the game longer.

Tomorrow was Christmas eve and I still had so much work to do. I promised that I would be home for Christmas, but there was still too much work to be done. I had to keep my daily pattern unpredictable so the feds wouldn't be able to keep up with me. If there was one thing I learned off watching all those investigations on TV, is they look for weak links and routines first. I steered clear of both.

"You want to go back to the apartments, right?" Valencia asked while we waited at a red light on Peachtree Avenue.

"Nah, I got to make a few stops. Just get off on Candler Road and I'll tell you where to go from there."

"Alright, I got you, boss." She responded respectfully.

She was a green woman from a small town in Tennessee. Handsome met her at a festival downtown a few months ago. She was on vacation with her friends. He introduced her to our lifestyle and she'd been property of DG ever since. She was a pretty woman that was looking for love in the wrong places.

"Aye, Vee. You want to start getting paid for driving me around?"

She shrugged her shoulders. "I mean, you know I don't need money. My father gives me enough to be comfortable, but then again, the Dinero Girls always asking me for stuff. I give it to them, so that doesn't leave me with much." She informed jokingly. "I guess I'll do it if you need me."

"Aight, its gone be long hours, though. I'm just telling you now. Sometimes, we might be gone for days at a time."

"It's okay, Toe-Tag. I don't mind as long as you promise to keep me safe."

"I got you lil' mamma."

I walked inside of the Western Union on Candler Road by myself. I walked right past the line and up to the ugly duckling at the counter. "Where Slim at?" Mr. Slim was the owner of the place.

"He in the back in his office. He's been waiting on you."

I lifted the counter up, walked behind it, and down the hall to Mr. Slim's office. When I got to the last door on the right, I knocked on it. "Come in!"

I walked in the small office while unzipping my Balmain jacket. I took a seat on the other side of his small desk. "Wassup, Slim? Everything good this week?

He shook his head sadly. "I was on my way to take my deposits to the bank, when some kids ran up on me and robbed me for my bag."

I looked at him curiously. "You told them you was under DG protection?"

"Of course. That's the first thing I screamed."

I nodded my head. "You notice any of them?"

"No, but I'm betting they're from around the area." He reached down and pulled out a shelf on his desk and came up with a small bundle of 20's. "That's my $400 for the week."

I waved my hand dismissively. "You paying for protection and you got robbed this week. This week is on me. Keep your money. I'm gone find out who did this and make an example out of them. It won't happen again."

"Thank you, young man. It's like the purge out here these days. Nobody cares about anything."

"All you can try to do is stay safe and you picked the right security company. I got you, Pops. That's my word."

***

I did my rounds throughout DeKalb County and the city of Decatur, collecting from different establishments, both legal and illegal. Just like Mr. Slim said, shit wasn't safe and everybody needs protection. Security always was, and will continue to be, one of the most needed services on earth. You sleep better knowing your shit is secured.

I had Valencia take me back to the hood so I could split this shit up with Rampage. Jasmine let me into the apartment with a see-through cheetah print body suit on. "Put on some muthafuckin' clothes. Nigga ain't trying to see that shit." I spat as I walked past her.

"Tell that to Rampage. He the one that made me put this shit on with his freaky ass."

"Shut the fuck up." Rampage spat while blowing a thick cloud of smoke up to the ceiling from the couch. "Toe-Tag, wassup my nigga? What you got in the bag?"

I sat next to him on the couch. "You know what I got in the bag." I opened the bag and pulled out all the money.

"How much is that?"

"We gone find out once we count this shit."

"We got to buy a money counter or some shit."

"Stop complaining nigga and help me count the money."

When we were finished counting, I separated the money into three piles. One for me, one for him, and one for the camp. "How much is in the pot for the camp?"

I shrugged my shoulders. "I don't know. I'm letting Monster hold that shit."

"Make sure everything accounted for."

I looked at him sideways. "You don't trust Monster?"

"I trust Monster. I just don't trust the demons inside of him."

"That's crazy If he heard you say that, he would spazz on you."

"I already told him. That's why he ain't been fuckin' with me like that lately."

"Nah, you know why he ain't been fuckin' with you?"

"Why?"

"You really letting that made man shit get to yo' head on the low."

He looked at me with a mug. "What? How?"

"It's hard to explain, but I see it. Monster see it too. You starting to change bro."

"Nigga, I ain't nothing like AK used to be. You got me fucked up!"

I sucked my teeth. "Stupid ass nigga, I ain't never say you was like AK, but you ain't like the Rampage I know either. You turning into somebody else."

"Yeah, nigga. A made man. All this money, fame, and respect. What you expect?"

"I don't know, man. Shit just don't feel right. I can't explain it."

He looked dead at me and nodded his head in understanding. "I think I do, though. Shit don't feel right because you ain't in my spot."

"That's how you think about me?" I asked in disbelief. All the shit we done been through and did for each other, this nigga really thought I was jealous of him and trying to take his spot.

"You gave your opinion. I gave mine." He spat matter of factly.

I stood up and put two stacks of the money in the book bag. "You lame as fuck for that one, but I'll catch you around." I said before leaving out of there before I said or did something I would regret.

CHAPTER 20
~ Kapo ~

I leaned on the rail next to Masio. I invited him out to Vegas for a night of fun, on me. I paid for his flight on a private jet and all. I've learned early in the game that it's smartest to keep your enemies close. He made himself an enemy of mine when he showed that he didn't respect my retirement and dragged me deeper in the game.

We looked down at the party goers enjoying themselves on the dancefloor. We were at this huge club that catered to the urban crowd. The VIP booth we were in gave us literally a bird's eye view of the whole place.

"I tried to get 2-Tall to deal with you personally, but he won't deal with nothing but Godfathers." He informed while scanning the crowd through his black Gucci shades.

2-Tall was the Godfather of New York. He supplied Dilluminati with Cocaine that he got from the Mendez Cartel Family. He lucked up and started dating, Malina Mendez. She was the niece of, George Mendez, the leader of the cartel. He was currently one of the most powerful men in the country.

I was glad he wouldn't meet with me because I didn't need that kind of heat on me. It's already bad enough being labeled a kingpin, but being labeled a drug lord is a whole different story. Of course, I had to play shit off, though. "Damn, that's crazy."

"I know. He be on a nigga bumper too. Want a nigga to associate with the rest of the Godfathers across the country and all that shit. I ain't friendly. I don't want to talk to them niggas." He complained.

"Sometimes, you don't get a say so, but I don't have to tell you that. You already know."

He laughed and looked over at me. "You got jokes?"

"I'm just saying."

He looked back down at the crowd.

"So, what plans do you have for the future of the family?"

He shrugged his shoulders. "I don't plan for the future. I just live for the day because tomorrow's not promised. Especially, for niggas as deep in the game as we are. Somewhere in an office in downtown Atlanta, there's a big ass billboard with my picture on the top, yours right below mine, and the rest of the made men in our camp. Just like we got eyes and ears in the government, they got the same in Dilluminati."

I nodded my head in understanding, sporting a serious face. "I understand your philosophy, but with the money, power, and resources that we have at this level of the game, we can prevent our downfall. Become untouchable."

"They got Dinero in chains, my nigga. Ain't nobody untouchable."

"Dinero's the Godfather of all Godfathers and I respect him to the fullest, but the truth of the matter, is that he's young and stubborn. He could've became untouchable but refused to give the government their piece. 2-Tall got the game from the Cartel, now look at him. It's not what yo do it, it's how you do it."

Masio took his shades off and looked at me. "What's your point? What you trying to get to?"

"I'm just saying, with the right decisions, we can go far in the game."

"Your job is to make sure everything is in line and all money is paid. Other than that, it's none of your concern. Enjoy the life we live while we still have it."

I didn't respond to his last statement. I just continued to look down at the crowd with him. I just had to test the waters and see where his head was at. Some would call it mind games, but I called it procedure. It was a part of the game.

Later on that night, me and Masio went two separate ways. He had a flight to catch, and I planned on flying my family out to Vegas for Christmas. I had one stop to make before I took it in to my hotel room. There was this place called Laser Wars. It was an advanced laser tag establishment with three different fields to battle on. It was a major family and tourist attraction owned by the man that I came to see.

The place was bigger than the club that I had just left. There was more security than needed for a friendly place like this, but I guess nobody complained about extra security these days.

Me and my shadows were escorted to a restricted area of the establishment, and got on an elevator. The tour guide pressed the only bottom on the console, but I couldn't tell if we were going up or down. When the elevator doors opened, there was a big stylish room with one desk, and a man that sat behind it.

The man's name was David Woods. He was a healthy sized African American man, who started out gun trafficking until he began making huge profits investing in real estate, and legitimized himself into a professional businessman. I could relate to his story because, like me, he came from the hood and turned a negative into a great situation.

"DG Kapo. It's a pleasure to meet you." He said as he got up out of his chair and walked around his desk to shake my hand.

I looked up at him with a smile. "The pleasure is all mines, Mr. Woods."

"Please, call me David." He walked back around his desk and sat back down in his big stylish chair.

I took a seat while Glock and Bullet stood on either side of me.

"Sorry, I don't have more seats but I'm new around these parts, and don't usually have much company."

"It's alright. They prefer standing anyway. Plus, I won't be here long."

He nodded his bald head in understanding. "Nice suit and jacket by the way, but down to business. How can I help you?"

"Well, this meeting is to see how you can help yourself. Of course, I've done a little homework, and I don't understand why a man of your caliber chooses to kneel down to the Italians."

His demeanor became one of an uncomfortable man. He probably didn't expect for me to be so blunt. "I don't kneel down for anyone but Jesus."

"Then, you should've told them to suck your dick when they pulled up on you telling you that you had to pay to operate in Vegas."

"Easier said than done. This is their city. What was I supposed to do?"

"I mean, I could sit here and tell you what I would've did, but we're two different people. Plus, it won't change shit. What matters right now is what you do to make the future better for you."

"What's your purpose, if you don't mind me asking."

"I came to offer you a proposal. A spot in the Dilluminati empire."

He shook his head. "DG has a certain image and it's the same image I'm running from. I really took a risk even meeting with you."

"Your still being investigated by the feds. How do you think I picked up on your trail in the first place? I got a few eyes on their side of the fence. So should you."

"That doesn't make any sense. I'm all the way legit now."

"Once you're on their radar for some illegal shit, you'll never be all the way legit. They'll always assume you're doing something behind the scenes, and whatever you're doing legally is just to cover that up."

"What about the Italians? I'll stop paying them, then what?"

"You'll continue to pay them for another two months until I get all my affairs lined up out here. Right now, isn't the time."

"So, you want me to stop paying them to start paying you?"

I shook my head. "I want you to stop paying them and invest in me. Big difference."

Malik D. Rice

CHAPTER 21
~ Rampage ~

"We've got to use one of the girls that don't got the logo tatted on them. I don't want this to get traced back to us." I said to Purp.

He gave me a knowing look.

"Man, I know you got a hoe in the cut that you ain't stamped all the way yet."

"Yeah, but they ain't trained. I ain't about to use no untrained hoe on no high-profile mission like this. I don't even know why Vonte targeting a nigga like this."

"Shit, me neither. That ain't my concern, though. The only thing I'm worried about is getting the job done so I can be out of Vonte's debt."

"You trying to use one of my hoes to reel him in, right?"

I nodded impatiently.

"Why you just don't catch him slippin' and snatch him up."

I looked at him blankly. "Nigga, that's what we do. You think I ain't think about that first?"

"I'll see what I can do and get back to you. Shit gone cost you, though."

"Money ain't a problem."

We dapped each other up and he exited my truck that was parked in front of his apartment building in the Park of Bouldercrest Apartments.

"Where to now?" Black asked me while starting the car back up.

I breathed a deep breath. "Just drive, my nigga."

I just wanted to clear my mind. Shit was so complicated for a nigga lately that I just wanted to say fuck it, but I know that people were depending on me that I couldn't let down. Usually, I would call Toe-Tag and get a little advice and encouraging words from him, but he been tripping lately. I wasn't into kissing ass and he knew that about me.

"Turn that shit up!" I told Black. It was a song from DG Bally called 'Da Top'.

I sung along to the lyrics, while nodding my head to the beat. He talked about how everything changes when you reach the top and how nothing goes as planned. I related to the song, plus his flow was off the chain. It was too bad he quit rapping. He'd been off the grid for a little while now. I was thinking about pulling one of those stunts, but it wasn't in me. The streets needed me and I was going to be there.

Black stopped at a red light. I sat back in my seat and pulled a pre rolled blunt of weed out of a Swisher Sweet box. As soon as I blew out the first series of smoke, three SUV's surrounded us. One from the back, front, and side. We had no way out. Plain clothed agents hopped out of the trucks and stood outside of our truck with guns in hand.

"Damn!" I said while taking another pull from the blunt, but this one was harder. Most niggas would've put it out, and started panicking, but I was really like what's the point.

One of the agents knocked on Black's window, and motioned for him to get out. He got out, and an agent got in the back with me.

He was a short stump of a man about four inches away from being a midget. That, along with his big head and pale skin, made him look very unusual.

I chuckled. "Either, it's the weed, or you a funny lookin' ass nigga."

"I think it's just the weed. They were right about one thing in your file, you are one arrogant bastard." He noted matter of factly.

"I take it you ain't here to put cuffs on me, because they would've already been on me by now. What can I do for you, short stuff?"

He reached in his shoulder holster, grabbed his pistol and hit me in the head with the butt of it so fast that I didn't see it coming.

"Fuck nigga!" By the time I grabbed my MP5 and brought it around towards him, his service weapon was dead in my face.

"This is a rumble you won't win, young man. Now, put it up and stop with the name calling."

Despite my anger, bloody face, and bruised ego, I did the smart thing and put the gun back on the floor. "What the fuck you want?"

"I want peace in America, but it doesn't seem like that's going to happen."

I wiped my face with my sweatshirt, and gave him a look that could kill. My head was throbbing and my vision was slightly blurred.

"I'm here to give you a proposal. You are a made man, but on a low scale. We're not necessarily interested in taking you down. We rather bag the bigger fish when possible."

"Ain't no way you waisted yo' time like this! It don't say solid nigga in my file?"

He shook his head disappointedly. "Your young with a whole future ahead of you. Think about your options. We only want Vonte. You help us bring him down and you walk free."

"You can walk yo' ass back to yo' truck because ain't shit going on."

"Everybody's so tough until we come swarming in with federal indictments."

"Suck my dick!" I spat without thinking about the consequences.

The next thing I knew, I was taking more blows to the head and face from the butt of his gun.

I woke up in Grady Hospital with Kamya and Babie standing over me. Both with tears in their eyes. "Damn, I look that bad?" I asked weakly.

Kamya shook her head no, but Babie nodded her head yes. I knew who was telling the truth. That little fuck nigga must've did a number on me.

"Where Black at?" I asked, hoping they ain't beat my nigga on the strength of me.

"He in another room looking like you." Babie answered weakly while Kamya just sobbed.

They'd never saw me this fucked up and helpless before and it fucked with me. Not to mention, the fact that Black was banged up in a hospital bed because of me.

"Anybody else here?"

"The whole damn hood out there mad as fuck and ready to kill somethin'. They want to know who did this to y'all."

"Where Toe-Tag at?"

"He out there."

"Go get him."

"Jasmine said she wanted to see you when you woke up." Kamya informed in between sobs.

"She can wait, y'all go get Toe-Tag."

The nurse had to come check on me and do all that extra doctor shit before I could have additional visitors. Toe-Tag walked into the room looking like the devil's son. The mug he sported when he saw me hurt my feelings. My nigga shed a tear, and I knew shit was real. "Who the fuck did this? They whole family gone! That's on the 4s."

"We gone have to chalk this one up." I didn't know it was possible, but his mug got meaner.

"Fuck you mean, chalk it up? They must've hit you in the head real good?"

"What I'm trying to tell you is that they is the FBI, nigga."

He looked even more confused than before. "They playin' dirty like that?"

"Yeah. I really did it to myself talkin' all that shit."

"What they wanted?"

"For me to tell on Vonte. I told them to suck my dick."

He nodded his head. "You ain't do nothin' wrong. What you want me to do?"

"Hold shit down. You in charge until I get off bed rest."

"I know Xavier on the waiting list, but you want me to handle the other two targets in the meantime?"

I thought about it. "Only if you positive it can be done. Be careful. I got a feeling the feds know more than what they supposed to. Shit might get real, real soon."

Malik D. Rice

CHAPTER 22
~ Jasmine ~

I walked inside of the hospital room, saw Rampage like that, and it literally broke my heart. I knew right then that I wanted him out of the game. I didn't want to lose him. In a way, he was all that I had. All that I wanted.

"Hey, baby." I said as I closed the distance between us.

He turned his head away from me, facing the TV on the wall. "I really don't want you seeing me like this."

"I'm just trying to be here for you. I know you in a fucked up mood right now, but please don't push me away."

He was silent for a long while and all I could do was stare at him. "You gone tell me who did this to you?"

Silence.

"I'm not trying to lose you to the grave or a prison."

Silence.

"Well, I guess I understand you not wanting to talk right now, but know that I love you, and I'll always be here no matter what happens." I turned around and started walking out of the room.

"Aye." He called after me.

I stopped and turned back around. "Yes, my King."

"Shit about to get real. If anything happen to me, I need you to make sure you take care of my sisters."

Karma was playing with herself on the couch next to me while I just looked at her blankly. My whole life, I wondered what went through a baby's mind. They stayed in their own world. I was in my own world but it was fucked up at the moment.

I sat back on the couch, rested my feet on the coffee table, and thought about how I could help Rampage. I felt so damn helpless. I picked up my phone and called Toe-Tag.

He answered on the third ring. "Wassup, sis? I'm busy so you got to make it quick."

"Is there anything I can do to help?"

He chuckled. "Have the apartment and that pussy clean for my nigga when he get out the hospital." Then, he hung up.

"Ain't that 'bout a bitch." I mumbled to myself.

I knew for a fact Rampage couldn't leave the game. Once you turned Dilluminati, it was what it was, but I still felt like there was something I could do to help. I just didn't know what. Maybe Toe-Tag was right. The only thing I could do was hold him down because I damn sure wasn't about to get in the streets and kill nobody.

I felt the strong urge to pray for him, but my relationship with God was fucked up. My mother always told me to praise Him because one day I would need, and go calling to him. I would roll my eyes on the outside and laugh on the inside, but sure enough, here I was with nobody else to turn to.

I got on my knees, faced the couch, and clasp my hands together. "Lord, I haven't prayed to you since I was a kid and I know you must be mad at me. I haven't been living right, and I choose to be around people who are living worse than me. I don't even know if you'll even listen to this prayer, but I'm going to try anyway. This prayer isn't about me, but this person effects my happiness tremendously. I need you to please shine your light on him. He's in a dark place right now and I'll follow him to the bottom of the earth, so I'm in the same place. I want you to please remove the nasty demons from his spirit. I can see them lurking in the shadows when I look into his eyes. My man is possessed and driven by the devil. Please, get him right so that we will have a chance at a bright future together, my Lord. It might not be the perfect future, but it'll be ours—" I didn't know what else to say so I just cut it short. "Amen."

After I put Karma to sleep, I don't know what possessed me to do it, but I picked up my iPad and just went to writing. At first, it was just random thoughts, and events, then a title popped up into my head. "Wife of A Demon." I said it aloud to see how it sounded.

Buddy started licking my big toe. I leaned down and scooped him up with one hand. "You like that, Buddy? You think I should write a book off that title?" He started going crazy from all the attention. "I take that as a yes."

I put him down and start typing away. Before I knew it, a few hours had passed, and I was starting the third chapter. I went on DGBooks.com and saw that they only required five chapters to submit your work for review, so I went back to work. I don't know where the passion for writing came from, but it came immediately after the prayer. It must've been a sign.

For the first time in a long time, I felt like I had a real purpose on this earth, and it felt good. Then, I started thinking about my mother. If I happened to get published, she would be proud of me again, and that filled me with more hope and motivation.

I wanted to call Rampage and tell him about my inner experience, but I had a strong feeling he wouldn't understand, so I brushed the idea off. He was my main motivation and I guess that was good enough.

Malik D. Rice

CHAPTER 23
~ Toe-Tag ~

"You sure you ready for this shit, lil' bro? This that grown man flow right here." Monster informed seriously.

I stood at the kitchen counter with him, ZyAsia, and her sister Missy, all waiting to see what I was going to do. They had all snorted a sizable line of cocaine, and only one remained. I looked down at the line of white powder as if it was a little alien break dancing on the counter.

"What the baby gone do?" Missy teased playfully.

"Shut the fuck up!" I spat defensively.

Monster put a hand on my shoulder. "Ain't nobody pressuring you, my nigga. You ain't got to do it if you don't want to."

"Nah, it was my idea." I took the straw, bent down, put it to my nose, and cleaned the line up off the counter like a champ. "Ohhhhh, shittttt! Damn!" I stumbled back and leaned on the stove for support.

All three of them stood around with goofy smiles on their faces and my stupid ass smiled back at them. I had never been that high. I never felt that good in my life.

"That shit right there give you superpowers, young buck." said Monster. "You ready to go handle this business?"

I nodded my head with a demonic look on my face. "Let's get it!"

"If a nigga look like he want to move, he die! I don't give a fuck who it is! If they in that room, it's the wrong place, wrong time! You hesitate to shoot; I'm gone shoot you." I barked at my brothers in the van.

We were parked down the street from a corner store on Gleenwood Avenue. It was an average convenient store to the public, but in the back, the owner held high stakes

Poker games for the get money niggas in the hood.

We masked-up and piled out the van with our assault rifles in our hands. It was raining heavily, which provided the perfect cover for us. I would've rather waited for after hours to hit the store, but the main target left early, so we had no choice. This was a hit and a robbery. We were killing two birds in one stone.

G-Baby was the first one in the store, and everybody else followed. Handsome and G-Baby fanned out to lay the customers and the clerk down to make sure they didn't go anywhere or do anything stupid. Me, Monster, and Dreek, kicked the back door to the gambling room and rushed in guns first.

"Y'all fuck niggas get right! Y'all know what it is!" I barked savagely, scanning the room while my eyes adjusted to the red light.

Monster slapped the nigga standing at the door with the back of his gun, spun it back around, and let a burst of hollows rip into his body.

Dreek was going around collecting everything of value, stuffing it into the book bag.

I spotted the target. He was the youngest nigga in the room and also the calmest. He didn't even look scared. I walked up behind him, grabbed his chair, and pulled it back, making him fall back to the ground.

He looked up at me, and before I could pull the trigger, there was gunfire in the front of the store. That was all the distraction he needed. He kicked me straight in the nuts, and tried to escape, but didn't make it anywhere. Monster cut him down at the door.

They helped me up and we went to the front to see what happened. I would've bet my saving's that one of mine had shot the clerk, or a customer, but never would I have thought that one of mine would be on the floor laying, and twitching, in his own blood.

"Fuck! Get him up! We can't leave him in here!" I commanded hysterically. I couldn't believe my little nigga was on the ground with holes in his body.

Handsome was on top of him, hugging him. "I turned my head for a second and the clerk shot him, bro! It's my fault, shawty!" He cried out. He knew he'd fucked up.

I looked behind the counter. The clerk looked to be dead, so I'm guessing Handsome handled shit accordingly, but I still pointed my gun at him and put eight more bullets in his body.

There were sirens in the background. "We got to go now!" Monster informed urgently.

I shook my head. "We can't leave G-Baby."

"We got to go now!" Monster grabbed me, and Dreek grabbed Handsome.

We barely escaped.

We all went back to Monster's apartment. "We lost one, but it wasn't our fault. You know shit happens in our line of work." Monster reasoned.

"You don't understand, nigga. Vonte said no fuck ups. We just fucked up!" I spat before taking another line of cocaine up my nose.

Handsome and Dreek were so stressed out, they hit the shit too. We didn't even count the money in the bag. We just sat down and plotted our next move.

"Y'all said y'all got the nigga y'all came for, right? He probably meant like make sure you don't miss the target. Plus, he an underboss He ain't gon' be tripping about a soldier dying in the field. It won't be the first nigga that died for him." ZyAsia chimed in while sitting on Monster's lap.

"Facts. We can cross the last two niggas out on this list and he ain't gone have shit to trip about."

I nodded my head in agreement, but deep down I had a feeling that Vonte was going to trip.

Later on that night, I was looking in the mirror after getting out of the shower. I had to wipe it off to get a clear view of the man in front of me. I stared him in the eyes and couldn't feel the connection I felt before. Of course, I knew the nigga because he was my best friend, but I didn't feel like I knew him. We used to have a good connection, now it was like we were two people.

Without warning, I swung hard, and punched him in his face. Glass shattered everywhere, and my hand was bleeding, but the good thing about it, was that the other nigga was gone.

Shanay came rushing into the bathroom, and looked at me with wide eyes. "Baby, what the fuck? What you got going on?"

I shook my head, grabbed a towel, and wrapped it around my hand. "Never thought shit was gon' be like this."

CHAPTER 24
~ Vonte ~

When Freddy summoned me for an emergency meeting, I already knew exactly what he wanted. We didn't talk business on phones, so I had to go all the way to his house in Dunwoody, Georgia. I was in Covington, Georgia when he had called me. Normally, I would've made him wait until I felt like resurfacing, but I knew what he was calling for, so I met with him.

He didn't have a castle on a hill. He laid his head at a classy suburban home in a nice little neighborhood. The houses ranged from $500,000 to a million dollars.

I parked my 2014 Chevy Camaro behind his smoke grey Maybach and went to the door. When I stepped on the welcome rug, he opened the door.

"Let's go back to the car." He spun me around and walked with me back to the car.

"Where we going?" I asked once I was behind the wheel.

"Just drive, nigga."

I pulled out of the driveway and hit the road. "Wassup, Unc'?"

"Don't Unc' me, nigga. I'm about ready to whack you. Please tell me why I'm getting pressure from the police and the Bloods about one of our soldiers dead on a crime scene that he should've never been on?"

I shrugged my shoulders with a serious expression etched on my face. "What you mean? Somebody in my camp? I ain't hear about none of mine dying."

He gave me a knowing look. "You know everything that go on in your camp."

"Man, just pay the police off and let me handle the Bloods. I'm in tune with all the big homies."

"I don't know what type of operation you got going on in that underworld of yours, but you need to get your shit together. If you gone play Harry Potter Chess, you need to have all your bases covered."

I glanced at him, then put my eyes back on the road. "Harry Potter Chess?"

"Yeah, nigga. You don't remember the one when they was on the chess pieces, and—" He looked up, saw the look I flashed him, and gave up. "Fuck it. Just know that this shit ain't no game. If you gone be playing these type of games, you got to be more efficient. If not, you get big messes like this. Now, you got to fix it. I got the police but you need to make some type of peace with the Bloods. This ain't the time for another war. I'm still trying to make the money back I lost during the last one."

"Just chill, man. Have I ever let you down?"

He couldn't say anything because he knew what I was capable of and how much respect I had in these streets.

The nigga that I had killed on Glenwood in the gambling spot was named Blow. He was a respected member of the G-Shine Blood set. It's crazy that this was the only one that Rampage fucked up on because it was the only hit on the list that was personal.

My mother fucked with younger dudes for some odd reason and ended up with this clown. He wasn't shit when he met her. She fell for him and started investing in him. Once he got right, he chunked the deuces and stopped dealing with her. I had to sit there and watch my mother go through that heartache. For that, I promised myself he would die, and he did. But now, I had to deal with G-Shine and they weren't the type of niggas I wanted a war with. They were on the east side with us, with twice our numbers. They were the killers who killed the killers.

I pulled up onto Glenwood Road in my Camaro with a truck full of shooters following close behind me. We drove into Victory Crossing Apartments and went to the back where Killa told me to meet him.

Killa was the 5th floor over G-Shine in the whole Glenwood area. We went to middle school together, and did some juvenile time together. We were even friends at once. We just went two different routes. But we both knew that we would both be boss niggas. Now, here we were, meeting back up under unfortunate circumstances.

"Gotdamn, Killa." I said to myself as I turned the corner of a building towards the dead end and seen nothing but red. It was about 50 Bloods all over the place spread out.

It was too late to retreat now. We drove into the storm. I got out and my kill team did the same. If their boss wasn't showing fear, why should they?"

For some reason, I wish it was daytime instead of 2:00am. Maybe, it was a chance I would walk out of here safe because knowing, Killa, it wasn't guaranteed. The only advantage I had was that I knew how he thought. He was a nigga just like me.

My boys stopped at a respectable distance and let me walk toward the middle of the street where Killa was waiting on me looking like a thugged out Dwyane Wade in a tailored, red, mink coat.

"Vonte. You been real busy in these streets lately." He greeted with a straight face. No handshake.

"Not really. You know how the streets like to boost shit up."

He looked me dead in the eyes. "Give me two reasons."

"For what?" I asked.

He shook his head. "No not what? Why? Give me a reason why you had my scrap killed, and most importantly, give me a reason why I should let you leave here tonight."

"I ain't have nobody whacked."

"Keep playin' with my intelligence, nigga. The only reason you still breathing is because my GF see a way to profit from this situation. Nobody win off a war."

"Talk to me."

"$500,000. And a drop on our shipment prices, but we'll discuss that later."

I like to laughed in his face. "We might as well crank the war up."

"You sure? I might as well kill you then, because Dilluminati gone whack you anyway nigga. We in the right!" He spat with a booming voice.

I slowly wiped his spittle from my face with a mug. I was up damn near $20 Million strong. What the fuck was $500,000? "Fuck it. Where you want that shit sent to?"

CHAPTER 25
~ Rampage ~

Jasmine was all up on me, trying to baby me and shit. "Get up off me, lil' girl."

"I'm just trying to make sure yo' ungrateful ass is comfortable." She countered angrily before storming off down the hall.

"Aye, Black. Get up." I said as loud as my broken jaw would allow me.

I was healing a little, but I wasn't all the way there. I just couldn't lay up in that hospital anymore. Neither could Black, which is why he was right there with me. We had at home nurses.

"What the fuck taking these niggas so long?" He whispered. He couldn't talk too loudly because he had two broken ribs. Shit, he couldn't even move without help. His little sister was in the back with Shanay. That was his at home nurse.

"Toe-Tag said he was on the way back from a mission when I talked to him. He said he was gone be here in 30 minutes."

Black cut his eyes at me. "That was a whole hour and some change ago. His lil' fuck ass scared to face me."

I just shook my head. I was in pain and spiritually drained. How the fuck did shit get so bad, so fast? Laying down in that hospital bed gave me time to reevaluate my life, and the lives that are affected just by my actions. I had to start thinking for other people, just not myself. Black was laid up next to me because of me. That wasn't cool.

And somehow, I feel like if I would've never ended up at the hospital, G-Baby would still be here. Black was laying there ready to blame Toe-Tag, but he was really supposed to be blaming me. He was like a little brother to me too and I felt fucked up about the whole situation.

Fifteen minutes later, Jasmine was letting Toe-Tag, and

Monster in the apartment. Monster took a seat, and Toe-Tag stayed standing looking down at us sadly. "Shit wasn't supposed to go down like that. G-Baby turned his back on the clerk, and got caught slippin'."

Black didn't say shit, just glared up at Toe-Tag menacingly. I knew he wasn't going to say anything, so I spoke my peace.

"Why the fuck you ain't take Quay instead of G-Baby?"

"Quay was the getaway driver."

"That lil' nigga was sixteen. Fuck you got him on a mission for?" Black asked weakly. All the strength was in his eyes and energy.

Toe-Tag sucked his teeth. "He was a soldier in the field, nigga. Why the fuck you acting like you ain't knowing what's goin' on?"

"Y'all niggas chill. Wassup with Xavier?" I asked, trying to change the subject.

He looked at, Monster, who reached in his pocket and came out with a black diamond ring. The same ring that Xavier had on in the picture that Vonte gave me of him.

"He in a better place now. I got an ass load of money and jewelry in a safe spot. We got to break Purp off, then split it up." He informed confidently.

"I got to get in contact with Vonte and let him know everything good."

Most of my injuries were facial and I didn't have problems moving around like Black, so I told Vonte that I would meet up with him for a meeting. I got dressed and had Toe-Tag drive me to the place where Vonte wanted to meet. It was right around the corner in the basketball court behind Sky Haven Elementary School. It was 11:00pm at night and the school was in a low key location, so I understood why he wanted to meet there. We never met at the same place twice.

"He must have some new jobs for us? It can't be that many

niggas on his hit list." Toe-Tag said while turning the corner by the school.

"He do deal with a lot of folks. Ain't no telling. If he do, you gone have to handle it. Matter of fact, stop the truck." I said.

He stopped the truck and turned around. "Talk to me, bro."

"Listen. I'm about to turn into a real Don, and fall all the way back. I'm gone need you to hold shit down, bruh. I don't care what you do, just make sure you take care of the camp, bro."

"You already know that. Why you telling me all this now, though?" He asked curiously.

I took a deep breath. "Just drive, bruh."

Malik D. Rice

CHAPTER 26
~ Toe-Tag ~

We pulled up into the park in the back of the school and just like we were expecting, Vonte was waiting on us with his kill team. All of them were outside of their trucks, just standing there waiting on us.

Vonte sat on top of one of the trucks looking like the Grim Reaper. He was in all black with a hoodie on and his dreads spilling down, covering his face. He sat there looking at us approach while smoking a blunt.

"I'm really tired of this nigga." I thought aloud.

"You better get used to him." Rampage said. We had to ride with the music off, so I could hear him talk.

"What's that supposed to mean?"

He didn't answer me. He just opened the door and got out of the car. "Let's go."

He was acting weird, but wouldn't tell me why. I didn't have time to think about it at the moment. I just got out the car, and walked up to Vonte behind him.

Vonte remained on the top of the car. I guess he was going to hold the meeting like this. It probably made him feel like he was sitting on a throne looking down on us like that. "I see y'all lil' niggas handled that business. I got to give it to y'all. How much y'all made on the backend?"

"We came out nice." Rampage answered.

"That's good. I remember my uncle gave me my first list of targets. It was shorter than the one I gave y'all and I took a whole month to finish it. So, y'all niggas doing something right, but not everything."

"Like what?" Rampage asked uneasily.

Vonte flicked the blunt he was smoking. "Remember what I

told you before you left me at that meeting in Magic City, Rampage?"

Rampage shook his head. "Not for real. I was too caught up in the hype at the moment. I ain't even gone lie."

"Big mistake." Vonte said while shaking his head in disappointment.

The next thing I knew, I heard a booming sound echo and felt a spray of warm liquid onto my face. A few seconds after that, I found out that the blast came from Silent's Desert Eagle, and the warm liquid on my face was Rampage's blood, along with particles from his brain. I looked down at my nigga and almost threw up. Half of his face was literally missing. A face that I've been looking at my whole life. A face that I would've killed for.

"What the fuck?" I bellowed as I reached down to my pocket for my Glock, but one nigga put me in a chokehold. A bigger nigga sent a breathtaking blow to my stomach. I fell down to the ground next to Rampage gasping for air.

Vonte laughed devilishly. "You fuck up, you get whacked. You get caught; you get whacked. You in the big leagues now, ain't no room for mistakes. Those are the exact words I told that lil' nigga before he walked up out of that strip club. He was in the hospital when that shit happened at the gambling spot, and he let you take shit over. You fucked up, not him, but I still whacked him because he was in charge of the camp, not you. The same thing I told him, now goes for you. Learn from his mistakes, don't let another nigga get you whacked. Make sure every job get done right, and never leave one of ours on a fuckin' scene. That's how shit get traced back to us."

He jumped off the truck and landed swiftly. "It's a trail across the street from the school. You got to follow the trail to the end, but be careful because it's a straight drop down at the end. That's where you gone drop Rampage body at. Anybody in yo' camp ask what happened to him, just tell them he wasn't loyal forever. You know how this shit go, and they do too. I would take a picture of you and put it on my page, but you a lil' rough right now, so I'll just take one off your page. You a made man now, lil' nigga. Hope you last in this shit." He hopped in the back of the truck he sat on, followed by the rest of his boys. They sped off the scene recklessly, leaving me alone with my dead best friend.

"Remember that time when we kicked our first door and a big ass dog was in the house? Nigga, I was scared as fuck. He was charging at me and he probably would've bit my face off, but you shot him. I'm gone miss you, my nigga. We wanted this life so bad, but look what it brought us. You dead and I just got robbed for my soul. This shit gone be hard without you, bro. What I'm gone tell—"

I thought about his little sisters looking up at me with tears in their eyes as I told them that they would never see their big brother again. Rampage was all they had. "I'm gone take care of yo' sisters, my nigga. That's on the 4s."

I said a quick silent prayer for my nigga and pushed him down the drop. It was pitch black in the woods, and I never heard his body drop. I wondered if he was on the elevator to hell. "I got a feeling I'm right behind you, bro. Save me a spot."

I drove back to the hood at lightning speed. I ran lights, swerved through traffic, and skidded to a stop in front of my mother's apartment. I opened the door, and looked at my family on the couch all watching a movie together. They looked back at me in horror. I was yellow, so I knew they saw Rampage's blood all over my face, and neck, really good.

Before any of them could ask me what happened, I fell to my knees. "Agggggggghhhhhh!" I yelled at the top of my lungs, before falling back on my ass with my head in between my arms, and bent legs. Then, I let out the tears that I've been forcing back for the past two weeks.

They all came running to me and embraced me. They knew it was serious because I was covered in blood, and plus, I never let anyone see me cry since I was eight. I sobbed uncontrollably. I just let it all out. I was so spiritually tired, and drained. I felt so empty inside.

Shit wasn't supposed to be like this. I kept thinking of a way out, but the truth was simple. There was only one way out, and I wasn't ready to die yet. I had to live for my family. The only way I was going to survive is to become just as heartless as Vonte was.

CHAPTER 27
~ Kapo ~

I kind of felt bad about the little nigga, Rampage. I felt like if I would've kept him under my wing, he would've never got whacked, but then again, how was I going to save him from Vonte? That young nigga there was definitely an extension of the devil. All I could do was pray for Rampage, and steer clear of Vonte. I wanted nothing to do with him, or his uncle, but unfortunately, I had to deal with Freddy.

I had to take my mind off the underworld for a moment because I had a meeting with my acquisition team in a midtown office I rented just for this occasion. It was very impersonal, but professional, and that's the image I was shooting for. They did homework on all of their clients, so they knew who I was, and what I was about, but that didn't stop them because I had access to the almighty dollar.

My acquisition team consisted of a business lawyer, financial advisor, and an accountant. All three of them had assistants that would most likely do most of the work, but they would make sure everything was in line and that's what I needed.

All three of them were seated on the other side of the desk I sat behind, waiting on me to begin. "I want to thank all three of you for joining me here today. I've hired each of you separately for different jobs, but you all will serve the same purpose. You are here to ensure the elevation and success of the legal empire I'm trying to build."

"You." I pointed at a geeky looking Asian woman that sat in the middle. She was the financial advisor. "Give me a good number to start off with."

She looked at me confusingly. "You have to specify your business. You have to give me a layout of all your legal financial dealings and then I'll let you know what I think you should do from there if I feel like money is being wasted, or misplaced."

"Look. I'm an intelligent man and well educated in a sense, but the truth is that I'm still learning about the actual business world. All I have to bring to the table at this point is money, and ideas. I wanted to start a chain of car dealerships, but I'm not so sure anymore. My sole goal is to just invest money into the most lucrative businesses."

All three of them nodded their heads. I guess they saw the picture I was trying to paint. "That'll be easier than actually trying to start your own businesses. The world of stocks and bonds are my specialty. And your starting number is entirely up to you. What can you afford?" She asked.

"$350,000 cash right now."

They nodded in unison again.

"What are you trying to invest into? You do know that an investment isn't guaranteed rite?" A balding black man with plenty of weight to spare asked me. He was the accountant.

"I really don't care if you invest in pepper spray, or oil, but I do need my investments to be guaranteed. So, if you don't strongly think that it'll return profit, don't put my money into it. Simple. I'm going to need y'all to work together on this. Money isn't an issue, plenty where mine comes from. I just need y'all to legalize the shit for me, and I'll pay y'all so much money that y'all won't care to take up anymore clients."

They nodded their heads more enthusiastically this time. I guess it was a professional thing.

A few minutes later, I had dismissed them, promising that I'd be in touch very soon. I loosened the tie around my neck, leaned back in my chair with my Mauri gators on the desk, and took a well needed deep breath.

Bullet stuck his head in the door. "Mr. Steward is requesting to see you again."

"Let him in."

Mr. Steward was a sophisticated looking white man that could've easily been a supermodel if he chose. He was the lawyer. "How can I help you?" I asked, sitting back up in my chair.

He waved his hand. "No need to get back uncomfortable on my account. I'm not here on official business anyway."

"Talk to me. You haven't said a word the whole meeting. Now, you have something to say? I want to hear it."

He took a seat in the same chair as before, and crossed his legs. "I think I have the answer to your problems."

"Talk to me."

"I'm aware that you're a certain type of businessman that's trying to legitimize himself, and there's nothing wrong with that, but Uncle Sam doesn't have to know everything."

He was earning my undivided attention. "Say, Glock!"

"How can I be of service, Boss?" He asked while standing in the doorway.

"Search him thoroughly for a wire." I commanded with my eyes still on Mr. Steward. "Don't take offense. Got to be careful these days."

He stood up, and submitted to the search.

"He's good, boss. Would you like me to take him to the bathroom for a more thorough search? You know technology is so advanced these days. There could be a small device somewhere complicated."

I took a long look at Mr. Steward. "Nah, I'll take my chances. Hope he doesn't make me regret it."

Glock left reluctantly and Mr. Steward sat back down. "Thank you for not taking me through the embarrassing process of a strip search. You have some very thorough security."

"It's the only way a man like me lives long." I grabbed my

bottle of Fiji water and took a sip. "You can carry on now."

"Well... Like I was saying, Uncle Sam doesn't need to know everything. I know a way to tuck your money away safely and securely."

I sighed. "I see you're not the kind of man that likes to get straight to the point."

"Sorry. What I'm getting to is the art of manipulating the overseas banking system."

The after meeting I had with Mr. Steward was way more uplifting than the one I had with the full acquisition team. He was going to end up making more money than the other two because he was thinking outside the box. He was a very ambitious buy. I could get far with him, but at the same time, I had to be careful with his type. He wouldn't know loyalty if it shot him in the face. If it came down to it, he would throw me to the wolves.

***

"Daddy! I been talking to you this whole time, and you ain't been listening?" My daughter, Kandice, asked heatedly.

We were having lunch at Zaxby's on Mount Zion Boulevard. She had me pick her up from the mall, so I just took her out to get something to eat. She loved Zaxby's, so I gave her what she wanted, like always.

"My bad, baby. I got so much going on in my head right now." I picked up a few fries and stuffed them in my mouth.

She pursed her pretty lips, and stared me down with those slanted eyes she got from her mother. I'm glad she got her looks from her mother because I would've been worried if she came out looking like me. "I know you ain't right here thinking about work while you on a date with me."

That got a smile out of me. "You letting niggas slide like that?"

"What you mean?" She asked confusingly with furrowed brows.

"You letting niggas take you on dates to Zaxby's?" I teased.

"There's nothing wrong with Zaxby's. At least, I'm not a McDonald's hoe." She said jokingly.

I put both hands in the air. "Thank God for that."

"You sound like you want me to fuck with one of them DG niggas."

I gave her a knowing look. "You know better than that."

"That's why you never let me talk to Rampage when I told you to hook us up?"

"Exactly. You see where he's at now."

"I think I would've been a better influence on him. If you would've let me talk to him, he would've still been here right now." She said with a trace of anger in her voice.

"You think so?" I asked while a chuckle.

"I know so."

"You don't know shit! That lil' nigga was the devil's son, and he was destined to fail. He was living too fucked up. You need to find you a good man."

"So, mamma get to have you, and I can't have no street nigga?"

I looked at her in amusement. "You can have a street nigga with some sense. Rampage wasn't the one."

"Okay. I'm gone hold you to that."

I shook my head sadly. My daughter wanted to be a Mob Wife so bad. Lucky me.

Malik D. Rice

CHAPTER 28
~ Jasmine ~

"You can stay in the apartment for as long as you want. Everything on Dilluminati." Toe-Tag promised.

"Thanks. Can I ask you a question?"

"What?"

"Do you think Rampage really loved me?" I asked curiously. It was something I needed to know.

He took a deep breath. "Rampage ain't even love himself. I got to go. Call me if you need something." He answered, then stated, before hanging up the phone.

I couldn't even be mad with his answer. At least, he didn't lie. I just wished shit was different. I mean, I always knew the day would come when Raylo never came home, but damn. I never knew it was going to be so soon.

All of Raylo's money, clothes, and jewelry went to Kamya, and Babie. I got to keep the apartment, Karma, and Buddy. Three responsibilities. At least, I would get to stay here for free. Plus, I had $6,000 left from the money Raylo gave me.

I heard Karma on the baby monitor, crying in her crib. "Here I come, mamma." I promised my man I was going to take care of this little girl, and that's what I planned on doing.

I went next door to pick Kamya up for our date. She'd been feeling so down lately over Raylo's death, I just wanted to cheer her up some. I offered to bring Babie with us, but she just wanted to sit around the house in a funk. Kamya didn't want to leave her, but she promised she would be okay.

I paid an old head in the hood to take us to South DeKalb Mall so we could watch the movie. Kamya wanted to see this new animated movie that had just came out about a little boy living life in the future. It didn't start for another hour, so we went to the food court to waist a little time.

She was picking through her Chinese food that she usually loved so much.

"Mya, please eat. I know you feeling down about your brother, but you have to eat."

She looked up at me with watery eyes. "I miss him, Jassy. Why did God take him away? He wasn't the goodest person, but he was my brother, and I needed him." She took a long breath with a serious face. "I hate Dilluminati!" She spat viciously. I never saw her so mad, and I never heard her say she hated anyone, or anything.

"It's going to be okay, baby. You want to move?"

She shook her head while wiping her tears away. "I would but I can't leave Babie. And she can't stand you."

"She don't like nobody. I just be so worried about you, Kamya. Who gone look after you now?"

Immediately after I asked that question, I remembered what Rampage told me in the hospital bed that night. *Shit about to get real. If anything happen to me, I need you to make sure you take care of my sisters.*

She shrugged her shoulders. "I guess me and Babie on our own."

"Y'all got me. I promised Raylo I would look after y'all. Why you just don't get Babie, and move out the hood. Rampage left y'all more than enough money."

"Because I feel safe in the hood. Everybody loves me there."

"You got a point there. I'm thinking about going back to school."

She seemed to brighten up at the thought of it. "You should. We can start sitting together at lunch time."

"I just might do that, baby. Let's go catch this movie of yours."

"Your nigga is the big dawg now. How does it feel?" I asked

Shanay.

We were sitting in the park behind my building. It was cold but we both invited the harsh winds. It seemed to match the harsh weather of our life lately.

She was sitting on the bottom of the slide. "Yeah, I know. It's scary, though. It seem like niggas don't last long at the top in this camp. Like we got a curse on us or something."

"They doing the devil's work. What you expect?"

Normally, she probably would've rolled her eyes at some shit like that, but now, she just sat there with a worried expression on her face. "This shit fucking Toe-Tag up in the head. It's killing him on the inside." She said the last sentence with a scratchy voice, like she was on the verge of crying.

I walked up to her and sat on her lap with an arm around her neck. "It's okay, baby. All you can do is pray for him and be there for yo' nigga."

"And how that work out for you?"

I couldn't say anything. I felt kind of offended, but I knew she was going through a lot, so I let it go. "I'm thinking about submitting these five chapters of my book to DG Books."

"Shoot for your dreams, girl. I hope you go on and do something with your life. Make your mamma proud."

I thought about what she said. Lately, I've been so stuck on making Rampage proud that forgot all about my mother. She didn't even know that I had started writing a book. I promised myself right then that I would build a better relationship with my mother because she was one of the few people on earth that really cared about me.

"Thanks you. I will. You need to find something you good at instead of sitting around worrying about Tee all day."

She waved me off. "I'm a Mob Wife. Nothing more, nothing less."

"You got so much more potential, Shanay."

"And so does, Tee. If my nigga wastes his life, I'm gone waste mine right along with him."

I just shook my head. It's a shame how much wasted potential was in the hood. I wasn't going to end up a statistic. I was going to make something of myself, and make my mother proud. Starting with this publishing deal I knew I had on the way. From this day forward, I planned on being focused on success. Productivity is key.

I'm gone make you proud, Raylo. I thought while looking at the ground down at him. I wondered if he was suffering just as bad as he was suffering up here on earth, or did the devil have him living it up. The thought scared me. I hope Adalis was wrong because I didn't want to go down there with him. It just hit me that I don't love him that much.

CHAPTER 29
~ Quay ~

"You need to cut that damn afro off your head. Who rocks an afro with a damn bald spot in the middle?" Monique said trying to make me mad as usual with her bitter ass.

I stood up off the couch and put my hoodie back over my head. "I'm the same nigga that fucked all your groupie ass friends."

"The only reason you fucked those thots is because you got that DG shit in your face, and you used to hang with Rampage."

I stuck my middle finger up at her, and left her apartment while slamming the door on my way out. I had business to attend to anyway. It wasn't anything else going on anyway, might as well make some money.

"Quay! Bring yo' muthafuckin' sorry ass over here!"

I didn't even have to squint my eyes to see who that was. I knew the voice too good. It was Bernice. One of my ratchet ass baby mothers. She was walking up to me, rolling her neck like a bobble head. "What you want, lil' girl? I just gave you some money the other day."

She waved me off. "Ain't nobody worried about yo' money, boy. I'm straight."

"Then, what the hell you want, man?"

She hesitated for a moment. "I been dealing with this nigga lately. He flexing all types of money on a bitch."

"You been workin' on him?" I asked interestingly. I knew exactly where she was going with this.

She nodded her head. "Hell yeah. Got the nigga wide open."

"I take it, he ain't seen you yet." I joked while looking at her messed up hair.

"Yes, I did. While you being funny. I been talking to the nigga for like three weeks. I had to make sure he was about what he was talking about."

"Why he ain't get your hair done?"

"Nigga you worried about the wrong thing! I'm about to get my shit done tonight by my cousin's daddy baby mother, and pocket most of the money he gave me to get it done. He supposed to be taking me out to the club, then after that, the nigga finally gone take me to his house."

A smile formed on my face. "Where he been fucking you at, then? His car?"

"How you know I gave him some pussy already, nigga?" She asked after punching me in my chest.

"Because I know you."

She rolled her fake hazel eyes. "He took me to a hotel for your information."

"Aight. Look. Keep doing what you doing. Who the nigga connected with?"

"I don't know. Why?"

"Because you can't just take anybody off. If he getting money in these streets, he connected to somebody. You need to find out to who. Get him drunk or some shit, and get him to talking. Let me know what you come up with." I started walking off toward my black 2011 Audi.

"Where you going?" She asked with a hand on her wide hip.

"Clock that nigga, not me." I got in my car, and burned rubber on her stupid ass.

Turk was an enforcer for PDE and a good friend of mine. We went to the same schools, and played in the same circles. We still kept in contact for various reasons. I met him in Paradise East Apartments on Bouldercrest, where he could be found the most.

He was in the breezeway sitting on the stairs with two females with him. "Lil' Quay. Wassup nigga?" He asked, as we did the DGPDE handshake.

"Same shit. Why you out here posted like a block boy?" I asked curiously.

"The soldiers more loyal to me 'cause they see my face more." He philosophized. "You gone handle that for me?"

I gave him a knowing look. "You know I wouldn't be standing here if I wasn't gone do it."

"You don't even know what it is."

"But I know you, and I trust that you ain't gone try to send me on no dummy mission."

He flashed a bright smile showing his solid gold teeth. "Would I ever."

"To another nigga, maybe, but I can't see you doing it to me."

"I'm glad you got faith in me. This a big one right here, too. Just got to do it exactly how I tell you—"

The funny thing about life is that you never know when, or where, danger is coming. You just have to live your best life, and cherish the good times. It looked like Stacy was doing just that. Everybody knew Stacy around the hood because her father, Pastor Dublin, owned one of those big churches that played services on TV. The church was all the way in Stockbridge, Georgia, but Stacy stayed running around East Atlanta for some reason.

I found her in a local club called Nite Lite right off Moreland Avenue. She walked in with a group of bitches that I recognized from around the way. Some older, and some younger.

"Stacy swear she down with them hoes, but they most definitely using her for the money." Handsome said from the passenger's seat, watching them disappear into the small club.

"I guess that's what's going on these days because them Dinero Girls got Valencia in the headlock." I said while declining the seat back so I could lay back.

"They *had* her in the headlock. Toe-Tag got her in the headlock now."

I nodded my head. "You talk to Lingo?"

"Yeah. He doing aight. Put some money on his books and phone yesterday."

"Long as he keep it solid, he gone be good in there."

"He don't know no other way. How long you think they gone be in there?" He asked with a yawn.

"For a lil' minute. I'm about to go to sleep. Keep your eyes open."

He just shook his head, and took a deep breath. This was going to be a long night.

I woke up and looked at the clock. "Damn, they ain't came out yet?" I'd been sleep for three hours.

He looked at me with red eyes. Either he was really high, or really tired. I take it he was both. "Nigga, you know I would've woke you up if they came out. I'm about to say fuck it, and go in here and get her ass."

"You gone lay yo' ass back, and get some sleep. I'm gone watch the door."

He didn't even protest. He did exactly as I said. Not even five minutes later, he was snoring like an old man. I had to turn the music up a little bit. People were starting to leave the club. It was 2:30, and the place closed at 3:00, so I knew they were coming out soon. "Bring your ass on girl." I whispered to myself.

***

Ten minutes later, they came out of the club more hyper than they went in. They were jumping around, shaking their asses, drawing way too much attention to themselves for us to handle the business right here.

"Get yo' ass up, Handsome." I got myself together and cranked the car up.

Handsome got up, and immediately pulled his ski mask over his face. "We might as well get this shit out the way now." He suggested groggily but he was obviously ready for action.

"It's too risky right now."

"Tressel Tree is right around the corner. We got to do this shit now 'cause if they get in that car, ain't nothing guaranteed, but we got her ass right now."

"What if somebody try to play Captain Save-a-Hoe?"

"You'll see. Let's get this shit out the way, so I can go home to my bitch." He jumped out the car with his pistol in hand.

I took a deep breath, pulled my ski-mask over my face, and got out the car to join the party. Handsome put two bullets in the air to cause confusion, so we wouldn't stand out too much. We already knew the girls would run to the Toyota they came in, so we beat them there.

We snatched Stacy up, and made it out of the parking lot along with everybody else that was scrambling to leave. Handsome was behind the wheel now, and I was in the back putting zip ties around Stacy's hands that were behind her back.

"Please, don't kill me." She begged in a trembling voice. "My father has a lot of money. He will pay you, just please don't kill me."

"Shut the fuck up!" I spat viciously before taping her mouth up.

Little did she know, her father was the one that paid to get her little ass snatched up. He was fully aware of her dealings in the streets and didn't like it, so he came up with a plan with his wife to scare Stacy away from the streets.

Turk's grandmother went to Pastor Dublin's church. He knew all about what Turk had going on in the streets and thought that he would be the perfect person to get the job done. Turk took the money, even though he was tied up with other things, and just paid me to do it. Easiest $5,000 I ever made. It wouldn't take much to scare Stacy back straight.

"Bitch, you mumble again I'm gone take you to the wolves and let 'em rape you until next January!" I threatened grimly.

Shit. By the looks of things, she'd learned her lesson already.

CHAPTER 30
~ Toe-Tag ~

I found myself back at KINKY for the third night in a row. I sat back with my hand on my dick as I looked down at some random big booty bitch clean a line of cocaine up off the table with her nose. "Shit! Where you get this shit from, baby?" She asked after sitting back up wiping her nose with a serious expression on her face.

"You the police?" I asked with a raised brow.

"You got me fucked up." She spat defensively.

"Alright then, stop asking all them damn questions and put yo' mouth on this dick."

She looked at me like she wanted to say something about the way I was talking, but I saw her eyes avert down toward my chest where my chains were. The next thing I knew, my hand was on the back of her head, gripping a handful of her weave. My head shot back while she went to work.

The door opened, and booming music spilled in. She popped up, looking at Dreek standing in the doorway. "Strong here to see you."

"Let him in." I said while pushing her head back down on my dick.

Strong walked into the room and looked down at us. "Oh, shit! My bad." He attempted to walk back out the door.

"Man, bring yo' ass in here! You ain't never seen a hoe suck a nigga dick before?"

He turned back around, and reluctantly took a seat on the other couch. "That's $1,500 for the week right there." He informed while sitting a small bankroll on the table, next to the pile of coke, and weed, I had on the table.

"You sure you want to talk business around her?" He asked

uneasily.

"She's Dilluminati. She know the consequences if she talk. Wassup?"

He shook his head slightly like he had something on his chest, but it never came off. "I'm paying you for protection, right?"

"Yeah."

"Alright. I got a problem that I'm willing to pay you extra to solve for me."

I pulled the girl's face up, made her stand up, then sit back down, but this time it was on my dick. She started bouncing up and down on my wood and I leaned her over to the side so I could see Strong. "Tell me about this problem."

He hesitated for a moment. "It's this detective that's been breathing down my neck—"

I stopped him right there. "It's gone cost you $50,000 to whack an officer; I don't think you got that kind of bread."

"I got it."

"I'm gone need half upfront just because the nature of the mission."

"You can get the whole thing up front if you sure you can solve the problem. Money's not an issue."

"We'll talk soon. I'll set up another meeting." I said before putting my full concentration back on the nut that I was trying to catch.

I caught a bright idea as Strong walked out. "Say, Dreek!"

"Ya." He answered with his head inside the door.

"Go get, Veronica. I want her to join this party right here."

I recently had this nice apartment rented on Moreland Avenue for my mother and sister to stay in. Shanay was mad because we weren't the ones leaving the hood, but she would get over it like everything else. I walked into the apartment at about 6:30am. The sun was up and all. Shanay was in the kitchen making breakfast.

"You woke up just in time." I said groggily. I was tired as fuck and liked the thought of eating a meal before I took it in.

She spun around with a mean mug. "Fuck nigga, I ain't never been to sleep! I been up worrying about yo' stupid ass."

"Watch yo' mouth." I warned before walking down the hall toward the bathroom. I needed to wash the streets off me.

I immediately started stripping when I got in the bathroom. I had a long day ahead of me, and soon as I woke up from my nap, I would have to walk out the door. I wanted to get this part out of the way. Just as I was about to step in the water, Shanay, comes trying to open the door, but it was locked.

"Let me in, Tevin!"

"Go make my food, man!" I spat back while lathering my body with soap.

I thought she went to do as told, but I was wrong. She must've slid the lock with a butter knife because the door opened. She stormed in the bathroom like a SWAT team. "This right here ain't gone work!" She spat after snatching the shower curtain back.

I continued washing my ass like she wasn't even there.

"Tee, don't make me act a fool. Talk to me. You know I hate being ignored. You done shut a bitch all the way out."

I walked up under the water. "Ain't shit to talk about."

"You pushing a good girl away." She sounded like she was on the verge of crying.

I shrugged my shoulders. "Save yourself."

"I'm going to my mamma's house on the south side. You know how to get there if you want to see us." She walked out the bathroom and slammed the door.

I put both of my hands on the shower wall and just let the water fall down on me. Yesterday's dirt was coming off, but the pain wasn't budging. It wasn't going anywhere. If only it was that simple. I never thought I would get to the point in life where I couldn't even look in the mirror. Niggas made this shit look so good when I was a kid looking at the made men in the hood flaunt their wealth and suck up all the glory. That was me looking from the outside in.

I used to always say what I'd do if I was a made man, and always used to wonder how I would feel. I would've never expected it to be like this. I didn't feel shit, but pain. Rampage was gone, my sanity was on the way out the door, Shanay might as well get the hell on. She'll be better off without me. I didn't want to poison her life. I wanted her to take my son and make a good life for him. The only good thing about my newfound position is that I'll be able to provide the money to make sure that they're both straight. It was the least I could do.

Shanay must've already had her bags packed because I only spent thirty minutes in the bathroom, and she was long gone by the time I came out. I ate some of the food she made, then fell asleep on the couch. I was knocked the fuck out. I'd been up for three days, and finally got to crash.

I heard someone banging on the door and popped up like a piece of toast. "Who the fuck is it?" I asked angrily as I grabbed my AK74 off the floor and stormed toward the door.

"It's Satan, nigga. Open this muthafuckin' door! I been out here for five minutes."

I knew that voice from anywhere. It was Vonte. "Why the hell you pulling up on me unannounced? You supposed to set up a meeting with a made man."

He smiled at me with an amused look in his eyes, then stormed past me while brushing my shoulder in the process with Silent close on his trail.

"What you want, Vonte? You know I don't fuck with you." I said after closing the door back and walking back over to the couch.

He chuckled from the arm of the smaller couch. "You not

scared to talk to me like that?"

"What you gone do? Whack me? Go ahead. Be my guest."

"What about your mamma? Your sister? Your baby mamma? Your s—"

Before he could finish the last word, I stood up with my gun leveled to his face. "Fuck nigga, I'll kill you right now!" I knew he was about to blow because I was visioning his head bursting open like a grape.

"Then, what? I'll answer that question for you. Silent, here, is gone kill you, then gon' do the same to all those folks I just named, but the only difference is that their deaths won't be as quick as yours."

I wanted to just shoot this nigga so bad, but I didn't have a doubt in my mind that he was lying about what he said would happen after, so I did the smart thing and put the gun down.

He smiled an evil smile. "You smarter than Rampage. He probably would've whacked me out of emotion. Don't let your emotions be the end of you."

I let go a well needed breath. "What you want?"

"I got a job for you."

"How many niggas you need killed?" I asked dramatically. This nigga was on another level of evil. I used to think I was fucked up, but this nigga had a real serious problem. He had to be stopped.

He shook his head. "This ain't a nigga."

"Then, who is it?" I had to hear this.

"Kandice."

"Who the fuck is that?"

He laughed. "Kapo's daughter."

To Be Continued...
New to the Game 2
Coming Soon

181

Submission Guideline

Submit the first three chapters of your completed manuscript to ldpsubmissions@gmail.com, subject line: Your book's title. The manuscript must be in a .doc file and sent as an attachment. Document should be in Times New Roman, double spaced and in size 12 font. Also, provide your synopsis and full contact information. If sending multiple submissions, they must each be in a separate email.

Have a story but no way to send it electronically? You can still submit to LDP/Ca$h Presents. Send in the first three chapters, written or typed, of your completed manuscript to:

LDP: Submissions Dept
Po Box 870494
Mesquite, Tx 75187

DO NOT send original manuscript. Must be a duplicate.

Provide your synopsis and a cover letter containing your full contact information.

Thanks for considering LDP and Ca$h Presents.

New to the Game

Coming Soon from Lock Down Publications/Ca$h Presents

BOW DOWN TO MY GANGSTA
By **Ca$h**
TORN BETWEEN TWO
By **Coffee**
THE STREETS STAINED MY SOUL **II**
By **Marcellus Allen**
BLOOD OF A BOSS **VI**
SHADOWS OF THE GAME II
By **Askari**
LOYAL TO THE GAME **IV**
By **T.J. & Jelissa**
A DOPEBOY'S PRAYER **II**
By **Eddie "Wolf" Lee**
IF LOVING YOU IS WRONG... **III**
By **Jelissa**
TRUE SAVAGE **VII**
MIDNIGHT CARTEL II
DOPE BOY MAGIC III
By **Chris Green**
BLAST FOR ME **III**
DUFFLE BAG CARTEL **IV**
A SAVAGE DOPEBOY III
By **Ghost**
A HUSTLER'S DECEIT III

Malik D. Rice

KILL ZONE **II**

BAE BELONGS TO ME III

SOUL OF A MONSTER III

By **Aryanna**

THE COST OF LOYALTY **III**

By **Kweli**

CHAINED TO THE STREETS II

By **J-Blunt**

KING OF NEW YORK V

COKE KINGS IV

BORN HEARTLESS IV

By **T.J. Edwards**

GORILLAZ IN THE BAY V

De'Kari

THE STREETS ARE CALLING II

Duquie Wilson

KINGPIN KILLAZ IV

STREET KINGS III

PAID IN BLOOD III

CARTEL KILLAZ IV

Hood Rich

SINS OF A HUSTLA II

ASAD

TRIGGADALE III

Elijah R. Freeman

KINGZ OF THE GAME V

New to the Game

Playa Ray
SLAUGHTER GANG IV
RUTHLESS HEART II
By Willie Slaughter
THE HEART OF A SAVAGE II
By Jibril Williams
FUK SHYT II
By Blakk Diamond
THE DOPEMAN'S BODYGAURD II
By Tranay Adams
TRAP GOD II
By Troublesome
YAYO III
A SHOOTER'S AMBITION II
By S. Allen
GHOST MOB
Stilloan Robinson
KINGPIN DREAMS II
By Paper Boi Rari
CREAM
By Yolanda Moore
SON OF A DOPE FIEND II
By Renta
FOREVER GANGSTA II
By Adrian Dulan
LOYALTY AIN'T PROMISED

Malik D. Rice

By Keith Williams
THE PRICE YOU PAY FOR LOVE II
By Destiny Skai
THE LIFE OF A HOOD STAR
By Rashia Wilson
TOE TAGZ II
By Ah'Million
CONFESSIONS OF A GANGSTA II
By Nicholas Lock
PAID IN KARMA II
By **Meesha**
I'M NOTHING WITHOUT HIS LOVE II
By Monet Dragun
CAUGHT UP IN THE LIFE II
By Robert Baptiste
NEW TO THE GAME II
By **Malik D. Rice**

Available Now

RESTRAINING ORDER **I & II**
By **CA$H & Coffee**
LOVE KNOWS NO BOUNDARIES **I II & III**
By **Coffee**
RAISED AS A GOON I, II, III & IV

New to the Game

BRED BY THE SLUMS I, II, III

BLAST FOR ME I & II

ROTTEN TO THE CORE I II III

A BRONX TALE I, II, III

DUFFEL BAG CARTEL I II III

HEARTLESS GOON I II III IV

A SAVAGE DOPEBOY I II

HEARTLESS GOON I II III

DRUG LORDS I II III

By **Ghost**

LAY IT DOWN **I & II**

LAST OF A DYING BREED

BLOOD STAINS OF A SHOTTA I & II III

By **Jamaica**

LOYAL TO THE GAME

LOYAL TO THE GAME II

LOYAL TO THE GAME III

LIFE OF SIN I, II III

By **TJ & Jelissa**

BLOODY COMMAS I & II

SKI MASK CARTEL I II & III

KING OF NEW YORK I II,III IV

RISE TO POWER I II III

COKE KINGS I II III

BORN HEARTLESS I II III

By **T.J. Edwards**

IF LOVING HIM IS WRONG...I & II

LOVE ME EVEN WHEN IT HURTS I II III

By **Jelissa**

WHEN THE STREETS CLAP BACK I & II III

By **Jibril Williams**

A DISTINGUISHED THUG STOLE MY HEART I II & III

LOVE SHOULDN'T HURT I II III IV

RENEGADE BOYS I II III IV

PAID IN KARMA

By **Meesha**

A GANGSTER'S CODE I &, II III

A GANGSTER'S SYN I II III

THE SAVAGE LIFE I II III

CHAINED TO THE STREETS

By J-Blunt

PUSH IT TO THE LIMIT

By **Bre' Hayes**

BLOOD OF A BOSS **I, II, III, IV, V**

SHADOWS OF THE GAME

By **Askari**

THE STREETS BLEED MURDER **I, II & III**

THE HEART OF A GANGSTA I II& III

By **Jerry Jackson**

CUM FOR ME

CUM FOR ME 2

CUM FOR ME 3

New to the Game

CUM FOR ME 4

CUM FOR ME 5

An **LDP Erotica Collaboration**

BRIDE OF A HUSTLA **I II & II**

THE FETTI GIRLS **I, II& III**

CORRUPTED BY A GANGSTA I, II III, IV

BLINDED BY HIS LOVE

THE PRICE YOU PAY FOR LOVE

By **Destiny Skai**

WHEN A GOOD GIRL GOES BAD

By **Adrienne**

THE COST OF LOYALTY I II

By Kweli

A GANGSTER'S REVENGE **I II III & IV**

THE BOSS MAN'S DAUGHTERS

THE BOSS MAN'S DAUGHTERS II

THE BOSSMAN'S DAUGHTERS III

THE BOSSMAN'S DAUGHTERS IV

THE BOSS MAN'S DAUGHTERS **V**

A SAVAGE LOVE **I & II**

BAE BELONGS TO ME I II

A HUSTLER'S DECEIT I, II, III

WHAT BAD BITCHES DO I, II, III

SOUL OF A MONSTER I II

KILL ZONE

By **Aryanna**

A KINGPIN'S AMBITON

A KINGPIN'S AMBITION **II**

I MURDER FOR THE DOUGH

By **Ambitious**

TRUE SAVAGE

TRUE SAVAGE II

TRUE SAVAGE **III**

TRUE SAVAGE **IV**

TRUE SAVAGE **V**

TRUE SAVAGE **VI**

DOPE BOY MAGIC I, II

MIDNIGHT CARTEL

By **Chris Green**

A DOPEBOY'S PRAYER

By **Eddie "Wolf" Lee**

THE KING CARTEL **I, II & III**

By **Frank Gresham**

THESE NIGGAS AIN'T LOYAL **I, II & III**

By **Nikki Tee**

GANGSTA SHYT **I II &III**

By **CATO**

THE ULTIMATE BETRAYAL

By **Phoenix**

BOSS'N UP **I , II & III**

By **Royal Nicole**

I LOVE YOU TO DEATH

New to the Game

By Destiny J
I RIDE FOR MY HITTA
I STILL RIDE FOR MY HITTA
By **Misty Holt**
LOVE & CHASIN' PAPER
By **Qay Crockett**
TO DIE IN VAIN
SINS OF A HUSTLA
By **ASAD**
BROOKLYN HUSTLAZ
By **Boogsy Morina**
BROOKLYN ON LOCK I & II
By **Sonovia**
GANGSTA CITY
By **Teddy Duke**
A DRUG KING AND HIS DIAMOND I & II III
A DOPEMAN'S RICHES
HER MAN, MINE'S TOO I, II
CASH MONEY HO'S
By Nicole Goosby
TRAPHOUSE KING **I II & III**
KINGPIN KILLAZ I II III
STREET KINGS I II
PAID IN BLOOD **I II**
CARTEL KILLAZ I II III
By **Hood Rich**

Malik D. Rice

LIPSTICK KILLAH **I, II, III**

CRIME OF PASSION I II & III

By **Mimi**

STEADY MOBBN' **I, II, III**

THE STREETS STAINED MY SOUL

By **Marcellus Allen**

WHO SHOT YA **I, II, III**

SON OF A DOPE FIEND

Renta

GORILLAZ IN THE BAY **I II III IV**

DE'KARI

TRIGGADALE I II

Elijah R. Freeman

GOD BLESS THE TRAPPERS I, II, III

THESE SCANDALOUS STREETS I, II, III

FEAR MY GANGSTA I, II, III

THESE STREETS DON'T LOVE NOBODY I, II

BURY ME A G I, II, III, IV, V

A GANGSTA'S EMPIRE I, II, III, IV

THE DOPEMAN'S BODYGAURD

Tranay Adams

THE STREETS ARE CALLING

Duquie Wilson

MARRIED TO A BOSS… I II III

By Destiny Skai & Chris Green

KINGZ OF THE GAME I II III IV

New to the Game

Playa Ray
SLAUGHTER GANG I II III
RUTHLESS HEART
By Willie Slaughter
THE HEART OF A SAVAGE
By Jibril Williams
FUK SHYT
By Blakk Diamond
DON'T F#CK WITH MY HEART I II
By Linnea
ADDICTED TO THE DRAMA I II III
By Jamila
YAYO I II
A SHOOTER'S AMBITION
By S. Allen
TRAP GOD
By Troublesome
FOREVER GANGSTA
By Adrian Dulan
TOE TAGZ
By Ah'Million
KINGPIN DREAMS
By Paper Boi Rari
CONFESSIONS OF A GANGSTA
By Nicholas Lock
I'M NOTHING WITHOUT HIS LOVE

By Monet Dragun
CAUGHT UP IN THE LIFE
By Robert Baptiste
NEW TO THE GAME
By **Malik D. Rice**

BOOKS BY LDP'S CEO, CA$H

TRUST IN NO MAN

TRUST IN NO MAN 2

TRUST IN NO MAN 3

BONDED BY BLOOD

SHORTY GOT A THUG

THUGS CRY

THUGS CRY 2

THUGS CRY 3

TRUST NO BITCH

TRUST NO BITCH 2

TRUST NO BITCH 3

TIL MY CASKET DROPS

RESTRAINING ORDER

RESTRAINING ORDER 2

IN LOVE WITH A CONVICT

Coming Soon

BONDED BY BLOOD 2

BOW DOWN TO MY GANGSTA

Malik D. Rice

CPSIA information can be obtained
at www.ICGtesting.com
Printed in the USA
LVHW022152170720
661013LV00010B/677